CROSS CHECKED HEARTS
WYNCOTE WOLVES #1

CALI MELLE

Copyright © 2022 by Cali Melle

All rights reserved.

No part of this book may be reproduced in any form or by any electronic or mechanical means, including information storage and retrieval systems, without written permission from the author, except for the use of brief quotations in a book review. This book is a work of fiction and any resemblance to any person, living or dead, or any events or occurrences is purely coincidental. The characters and story lines are created purely by the author's imagination and are used fictitiously.

Cover Designer: Cat Imb, TRC Designs

Editor: Rumi Khan

To my husband... the hockey playing heartthrob who stole my heart and never gave it back.

PROLOGUE
ISLA

Two years ago

A low rumble of thunder comes from outside as a steady rain begins to fall from the night sky. I roll over in bed, looking out the window as droplets pelt against the panes of glass. A soft glow from my TV screen illuminates the room and the quiet sound of classical music sounds from the speakers.

It's well after midnight and my brother, August, still isn't back from the going-away party that was being thrown for him and his friends tonight. I was invited, but my parents were smart enough to keep me home. They know how those parties get, with a bunch of newly graduated high school jocks.

A part of me didn't want to go, anyway. I knew that *he* would be there and *she* would be there with him.

Logan Knight.

My brother's best friend.

August and I were only born two years and five months apart. Growing up, I idolized him and put him on a pedestal. Even though we were close in age, he was still my big brother and I looked up to him. The popular kid in school, the star hockey player. And because we were so close in age, his friends took me under their wings, treating me like their little sister too.

Everyone *except* Logan.

In front of everyone, he kept me at arm's length and acted like I was his little sister. When no one was looking, he would sneak into my room and hold me in his arms until the sun rose. He whispered his secrets into my soul and marked my skin with his lips. His light caresses and featherlike kisses were only for me to know about.

I was his dirty little secret.

At least, that's how it felt. Even though we never went any further than kissing, I was still his damn secret.

And now, this time tomorrow, Logan and my

brother will be off to a summerlong hockey camp before starting college. I've seen both of them almost every single day of my life. I don't know when I would see them again. Maybe Christmas break? Either way... instead of spending his last night with me, he was getting drunk with the hockey team and *her*.

Logan Knight was the second most popular kid in school. He wasn't the star hockey player, like my brother, but he was August's right-hand man. Even though he was moody and broody, he was the glue that held their team together. August was the sun, while Logan was the moon. He shone brighter than my brother, but only in the darkness.

I continue to stare out the window, listening to the sounds of the summer storm as it rolls in. The windowpanes are streaked with rain and lightning flashes in the distance. Tears prick the corners of my eyes and I blink rapidly against the burning sensation, willing them away. I can't cry, I *won't* cry.

A set of headlights shine from down the road, getting brighter as they move closer to the house. The light doesn't quite reach my windows, but it shifts and lights up the side of the house as the car pulls into our driveway. I can hear the bass from the music playing and a smile forms on my lips, knowing that it's August and that our parents will hear from the neighbors about this in the morning.

He always knows how to make a scene with his arrival and his presence is something that refuses to be ignored. The house already feels empty and lonely, knowing how quiet this summer will be without him and his friends taking over the house.

The music falls silent and I'm left with the sound of the storm outside and the music playing from my TV. The melody shifts into a slower tempo and my heart sinks as I hear a lone car door slamming shut. August comes into the house, but he's quiet as he makes his way to his bedroom and doesn't stop by mine to annoy me.

August quietly closes his bedroom door and I pull my covers closer to my chin. Logan was supposed to be with him, but he must have gone home with *her*. His girlfriend. I can't be mad at him for it. He's with her, not me.

I pull the comforter over my head and bury my face in the pillows as my teenage crush rips my heart to shreds. This is what I get for falling for someone who never felt the same way. All of the veiled glances and stolen kisses never meant a thing to him. I was just a distraction from the demands of Logan's life and nothing more.

My bedroom door opens, but the soft sound is muffled out from the comforter. I sigh, turning my head sideways on my pillow. "Go away, August." As much as I love my brother, I just want to be alone.

The door closes and just when I think that he left, I hear his light footsteps as he pads across my bedroom. The cold air from my bedroom touches the skin on my legs, sending a shiver through my body as the blankets are lifted up. He doesn't pull the comforter away from my head as he climbs under the covers.

"August," I groan, scrunching my face up as the smell of alcohol touches my nose. The mattress dips under his weight. "You smell like shit and I just want to be alone right now."

The smell of *his* cologne overwhelms my senses and my breath catches in my throat when realization muddles my brain. My heart beats erratically in my chest. It's not my brother. It's Logan.

I don't move, my body frozen in place as I hide under the comforter. Logan inches closer to me, his chest warm and solid as he presses it against my back. My skin prickles as his fingers trail along the sliver of my waist that is exposed from my tank top. He slides his soft palm along my flesh and wraps his arm around me.

"I missed you tonight," he breathes into my hair. The smell of whiskey is heavy on his breath. "Why didn't you come to the party at King's house?"

Hayden King. Everyone knows him as King, although he's more of a joker than anything. He's another one of August's best friends, but he isn't quite like Logan. They've been best friends since they were kids, but Logan and August were always attached at the hip.

"Because my parents wouldn't let me go."

"Bullshit," Logan chuckles, lightly tracing circles along my stomach. "Since when does Isla Whitley give a shit about what her parents say? Don't play innocent like you've never snuck out before."

I clench my jaw and swallow hard as I resist the urge to relax against him. My mind and my heart are at war and I'm caught in the middle of it all. "It wasn't my scene tonight."

"Well, all of the guys missed you." He pauses as he rests his forehead against the back of my head. "You know that we're all leaving tomorrow morning for camp."

"Yeah, I know," I grit out, my chest tightening at the painful reminder. His words hit a nerve and I instantly feel guilty for not going. They were all like family and I should have been there to say bye to everyone instead of letting my jealousy get to me. "Was Renee there?"

Logan falls silent for a moment, but his fingers don't stop moving across my stomach. "Yeah, why?"

I shrug against him, mentally kicking myself for even bringing up her name. Jealousy is something that I've struggled so hard with. Logan isn't mine—he never was mine. There's no reason to be feeling the pinch in my heart.

"Tell me why, Isla."

"I don't know," I mumble, shaking my head. "I figured you would have went home with her instead tonight."

Logan pulls his hand away from my stomach and brushes my hair away from my face. "I don't think she would have wanted to be anywhere near me tonight."

"Why's that?" I ask, my eyebrows pinching together as I roll onto my back. Logan shifts beside me, his midnight-colored hair hanging onto his forehead in tousled waves. The light from the TV illuminates through the white comforter and his blue eyes shine as he props his head on his hand and stares down at me.

His full lips curl, flashing his bright white teeth at me. "Because I broke up with her."

My eyes travel across his symmetrical face, memorizing every inch that is already stored in my brain. His sharp eyebrows, his chiseled jawline. I move my gaze over his straight nose—with a small bump on the bridge of it from taking a puck to the face—before settling back on his ocean blue eyes. "Why the hell did you do that?"

As much as I hated the thought of Logan and Renee together, it was all out of envy. I never had anything against Renee. In all honesty, she may have been one of the nicest people I've ever met. She just had something that I wanted, but I could never actually hate her.

Logan shrugs, flattening his palm along the side of my face. "I don't have time for a girlfriend right now. Especially one who is going to be on the other side of the country." He pauses, chewing on his bottom lip as he cups the side of my face. "I need to focus on hockey more than anything."

It feels like a punch to the gut, but I sigh at his brutal honesty. He has the same mindset as my brother—and while it might not be a bad thing, it still hurts. Nothing will ever come before hockey. That is his first love. Everything else just falls in line behind the stick and puck.

"You know that I'm going to miss you, right?"

"Yeah, right." I roll my eyes, swallowing hard over the emotion growing thicker in my throat. His words have the ability to warm my soul, but I know that they're just words. How could he possibly miss me? He won't miss me in the way I wish he would.

"Isla," he whispers, slowly stroking the side of my face as his eyes fall shut. "You just don't get it, do you?"

"What's to get?" I retort, attempting to hide the pain with a facade that's colder than the ice that he skates on. "You're leaving for college, Logan. You have so much ahead of you and you're going to kill it playing college hockey."

His eyes open, his bright blue irises staring directly into my eyes. "Yeah, I know, but that's not even what I'm talking about." He stops for a second, a wave of an unreadable emotion passing through his drunken eyes. "You are a constant in my life. And I hate the fact that I'm going to be leaving you. The fact that I won't see you almost every single day. I won't see you sitting in the stands, cheering me on at every game."

"Logan." I stop, pulling away from him slightly. I've already let my mind and my heart get so invested in a guy that wasn't mine. A guy that simply viewed me as a little sister, regardless of all the times he snuck into my bed or held my hand when no one was looking. "I'll always be a phone call away."

He shakes his head, not accepting that. "That's not the same. I'm going to miss you—this."

"I know what this really is." My voice is clipped and tears prick my eyes, threatening to spill at any given moment. "I'm your dirty little secret. You've always used me as a distraction and honestly, it feels pretty shitty thinking about how you've kept this hidden."

"You think your brother would be okay with this? Your parents? Shit, Isla… you're my best friend's little sister. You have to know that no one else would understand or accept this."

I narrow my eyes at him. "Since when do you give a shit about what anyone else thinks?"

"This is different," he insists, reaching for me again. "August is like my brother. Your parents are like my second parents. All of you are my fucking family."

"So, you think you could just play with my heart all of these years and it wouldn't affect me?" My voice cracks and the tears begin to fall. I don't even bother trying to stop them as they stream down the sides of my face. "That I wouldn't want something more than just this?"

"I never wanted to hurt you, Isla. That's exactly why I knew that we could never get involved." He sighs, the smell of whiskey skating across my face. "I'm no good for you. And I swore to myself that I would never be the one to tarnish your shine."

I face away from him, rolling toward the window. Staring outside, I watch as the rain steadily falls in tandem with the tears that fall from my face. It hurts—every last word that he speaks—but I know that it's the truth and sometimes the truth is a hard pill to swallow.

What was I thinking? That he broke up with Renee and it meant we would be together? No. I've been living too much in my head, in this little fantasy world I created. And it was something that would never be our reality.

"Isla. Don't cry, baby." Logan's voice is soft as he gently grabs my shoulder and rolls me onto my back. "This, between us, it was never just a distraction. I got greedy and wanted a taste of what we could have had if things would have been different."

"That's not even fair," I whisper as he brushes the tears away from my face. "You know, I've had a crush on you for as long as I could remember. And you gave me little bits and pieces of yourself, even if it was just a secret. I took it to heart and read into it more than I should have. I thought you felt the same way about me."

His hand falls still on the side of my face. "You think I don't feel the same way?" His face contorts in pain and his eyes are glazed over as he stares down at me. "The way I feel about you is the reason why I can't let this be anything."

My eyebrows pinch together as my eyes search his. "That makes no sense. If you felt the same way about me, you would want to—"

Logan silences me as his mouth collides with mine. His lips are soft and gentle, moving slowly against mine. The way he feels is ingrained in my brain and my soul. He cups the sides of my face as he moves closer, his chest pressing against mine.

I want to fight against him, to tell him that I'm not done talking, but he succeeds in chasing the thoughts away. With one touch, one swipe of his tongue along the seam of my lips, I turn into a puddle of mush on the bed. His body is warm against mine and he tastes like whiskey as he invades my mouth. His tongue dances with mine and I instinctively wrap my arms around his shoulders.

I want to stay like this with him forever, but I know it will never last. He confirmed it with everything he said and I know that when I wake up in the morning, he'll be gone. My only option now is to take what I can get from him—this one last time.

Logan kisses me deeply, and there's nothing rushed in the way his lips move against mine. He breathes me in like I'm the oxygen his body needs to survive and I give him every last breath. He's gentle and tender, stroking the sides of my face, like we have all the time in the world together. Like he's savoring the moment and imprinting this memory in his brain for after he leaves.

I move my hands away from his neck, sliding them down his torso. Beneath my palms, I feel the ridges of his muscles from countless hours of working out. I've seen him without a shirt before and his body is something that rivals fitness models'. He's not ripped, but he's fit and it's enough to make my mouth water.

My hands shake and my palms are damp as I slide my fingertips along the waistband of his sweatpants. Logan moans into my mouth, his tongue thrusting against mine before he pulls away. He lifts his head, staring down at me with his lips plump and red from kissing me.

"What are you doing?" Logan murmurs, his hand reaching down to grab mine. "Isla. Stop."

"Why?" I retort, attempting to pull my hand from his. "Isn't this what you really want? This is what Renee did, isn't it?"

"Isla, what the fuck?" His voice is harsh and he wraps his fingers around my hand as he jerks it up to his chest. "Just fucking stop it. This isn't what I want and stop worrying about Renee."

His rejection is a straight blow to the chest and my ego. Embarrassment fills me, heat creeping up my neck as it spreads across my cheeks. I want the mattress to open up and swallow me whole. My heart crawls into my throat and I want to disappear from how desperate and pathetic I just acted.

"You don't want me?"

Logan holds my hand to his chest and shifts his hips. I inhale sharply as I feel his erection press against my leg. "Of course I fucking do, but not like this."

"What if this is what I want?"

A ghost of a smile plays on his lips and the sadness of it touches his eyes. "Trust me, baby, you don't. You might think that you do right now, but I'm not going to take your innocence. Not like this."

"Just go, Logan." My voice is small and the pain

is evident in my words. I appreciate his respect and consideration, but that doesn't make it hurt less. "Please."

"And miss out on spending the night with my most favorite person in the world?" His lips curl upward into a true smile as he shakes his head. "Nope. I don't think so."

Logan rolls onto his back, pulling me along with him. I settle along his side, resting my head on his chest as he slides his arm under my neck. He envelops me, his hand on my shoulder as he holds me close. We're both silent, listening to the sounds of the rain falling outside and the classical music that plays from my TV.

"Logan?" I whisper his name, inhaling the scent of his cologne and the whiskey on his breath as he exhales softly. "Promise me that you won't forget about me after you leave."

"I could never forget you, even if I tried."

I tilt my head a little, looking up at him. "That wasn't a promise."

Logan chuckles softly as he plants his warm lips against my forehead, warming my soul.

"I promise."

CHAPTER ONE
ISLA

PRESENT

"Isla!" My mom's voice sounds from down the hall. Her heels click on the hardwood floor as she pushes my suitcases to the front door. "Your brother will be here any minute. Do you have all of your stuff?"

Grabbing my backpack, I throw it over my shoulder and give my bedroom a last farewell before heading down the stairs. "Yeah, I have everything packed. Although, I honestly think that I might have overpacked."

My mom is standing by the door as August strolls in with a bright smile on his face. The two of them look almost identical with their soft brown hair that is naturally wavy. Both of them look at me with their soft hazel eyes. "Are you sure that you don't want your father and I to help you get settled into your dorm?"

"Come on, Mom," August whines, wrapping his arm around the tops of her shoulders and pulling her against him. "You don't trust me to take care of my little sis?"

"I trust you, but this is a big day," she says, her voice cracking slightly as she sniffles. "Both of my kids are going to be out of the house and I don't know what I'm going to do with it being so quiet and empty here."

"Hey now," my dad interjects, stepping up behind me as he rests his hand on my shoulder. "Did you forget that your husband will still be here?"

August and I break out into a laugh as our mom shakes her head at our dad and sighs. "You know what I mean, Dennis. This is a big deal!"

"I know, I know," my dad says with a chuckle as he steps in front of me and pulls me in for a hug. "We're so proud of you, sweetheart."

"Thanks, Dad," I tell him, hugging him tightly before pulling away. The emotion wells in my throat and I swallow back the tears. I can't let myself cry. I'm not going away forever. Even though Wyncote

University is three hours away, I'm not that far away from them.

My mom breaks away from August, taking a step toward me with tears in her eyes as she embraces me tightly. "My baby," she murmurs, her voice cracking. "I can't believe you're finally off to college. I am insanely proud of you, sweet girl."

"You'll see me soon enough, Mom," I whisper, not fully trusting my voice. My parents have been such a constant in my life. It's one of the many things that I have to be grateful for in life. So many of our friends come from broken homes. But not August and I. We have a great family and parents that have always gone above and beyond for us.

My mom takes a step back, wiping the tears from her eyes before holding my face in her hands. "You call me as soon as you get there, okay? I need to make sure that you get there safely." She glances over her shoulder, narrowing her eyes at August. "We all know how your brother drives like he's a race car driver."

"Hey! That's not true." August smiles at our parents as they both give him a knowing look. "Okay, I might drive a *little* fast sometimes, but I'm still a safe driver."

"No dumb shit, August," my dad warns him. "Just get her there in one piece."

I walk over to August as he presses his hand over his chest. "The two of you wound me. You know that Isla isn't your only child. You do have a son too."

"Shut up," I laugh, punching him lightly in his firm shoulder. "You've been the apple of their eye for many years. Let me have this moment."

August slides the handles of my suitcases into his hands and lifts them effortlessly. I readjust the backpack on my shoulders as I turn back to my parents once more.

"The two of you better leave before I decide to keep you here forever." My mom smiles, her eyes wet with emotion. "We love you both!"

We bid our farewells to our parents and it's a bittersweet moment as I climb into August's car while he throws my suitcases into the trunk. He slams it shut and the car dips beneath his weight as he climbs into the driver's side. My eyes are glued to the house as he starts the engine and slowly backs out of the driveway.

This is the home that I've known my entire life. So many memories were made inside those walls and it feels strange, leaving it all behind. I know that I'll be back in a few months for winter break, but I'm stepping out of my comfort zone. There's a weird sense of excitement as we leave. I'm off to college, off to another chapter in my life.

August glances over at me as he slides his sunglasses over his eyes. His smile is infectious as he flashes his bright white teeth at me. "You ready for college, little sis?"

"I am," I admit, smiling back at him. "I'm just a little nervous. I don't really know anyone there and what if I don't make any friends?"

He shakes his head at me as he pulls out onto the main road, heading in the direction of the freeway. "Nonsense. You will most definitely make friends and you already have some there anyways. You know me and you know Logan."

My breath catches in my throat and I swallow hard over the knives lodged in my throat. I haven't seen Logan since the night they left the summer before college. Logan and August ended up getting an apartment near campus together. Not long after they started their first year, Logan's mom moved to the same city as them since she was pursuing her career as a sports agent.

There was no reason for Logan to come back to Clifton Falls since his mother was his only family. There was nothing left here for him... except me. He made a promise that he wouldn't forget about me, but given his absence, I think it's safe to say he broke that promise.

"How is Logan, anyways?" I ask my brother, attempting to keep my voice even and void of any emotion. He knows nothing of what had happened in the past with Logan and I have to keep it that way. I don't know how well August would take it and the last thing I want to do is come between them.

August shrugs as he eases the car onto the freeway. "You know how Logan is. He isn't exactly an open book, but he's been good. Mainly just focused on hockey and school." He pauses, glancing at me as a laugh rumbles in his chest. "Typical fucking Logan, right?"

I smile back at him, shaking my head as my heart clenches in my chest. "That sounds like the Logan we've always known."

I fight the urge to ask him if Logan is seeing anyone. When it really comes down to it, it's none of my business. And even though I asked him to promise me that he wouldn't forget about me, I couldn't expect him to not get involved with anyone else. He's a young guy in college. We were never together anyway, so that wouldn't be a realistic expectation or remotely fair to ask.

Logan was never mine.

And chances are he never will be.

It was easier to let go of my little obsession with him while he was gone. It had been almost two years and even though I still thought about him, I didn't have him around every day as a constant reminder of what I would never have. But now… now he's going to be back in my life again and I don't know how I'm going to completely let go.

"What's wrong, Isla?" August asks after we drive in silence for a few minutes. "You look like someone just killed your puppy or some shit."

I look over at him, giving him the middle finger. "I'm just nervous, okay?"

"I get it, trust me," August says softly with a sympathetic smile. "I promise, you will do fine. Like I said, you have me. I'll always have your back, even if you are annoying as hell sometimes."

"How can you be so nice, but such an asshole at the same time?"

August reaches for the volume knob and begins to turn it as the sound of rap begins to blare through the speakers. "I'm sorry! I can't hear you over the music!" The bass is so loud, it feels like it's rattling my brain, but then again, this is my brother. This is the shit I've missed from him.

Laughing to myself, I settle deeper into my seat and stare out the window as I watch the line of trees passing by us in a blur. "Such an asshole," I mumble to myself, letting my eyes fall shut. I let the music drown out my thoughts and the movement of the car lull me to sleep.

———

When I wake up, I notice that we aren't in front of the university. Instead, we're pulling up in front of a swanky-looking apartment building. I glance at August as he puts the car in park, directly in front of the massive structure. "What are we doing here?"

"Surprise!" August pushes his sunglasses up over his head with a smile forming on his lips. "You really think I was going to let you stay in the shitty dorms when we have an extra bedroom in our apartment?"

I stare back at him. "But I thought I was supposed to be staying on campus?"

"Nah," he says, shaking his head as he pushes open his door. "I ran it past Mom and Dad and they were cool with it. I told them not to say anything because I wanted it to be a surprise."

August climbs out of the car, softly shutting the door behind him, and I'm left staring at where he was just sitting. He rounds the back of the car and unloads my bags from the trunk. Coming to the same school that Logan attends was bad enough... but now I'm going to be living in their apartment too?

If only the ground would open up and swallow me whole. That would be pretty freaking great right now.

August stops by my window and the sound of his knuckles on the glass grabs my attention. I glance over at him, swallowing back my anxiety as I slowly open my door and climb out. "Come on. It's cold as fuck out here and your bags are heavy as hell."

I narrow my eyes at him. "You basically live at the ice rink and you're complaining about the temperature outside right now?"

He rolls his eyes, walking past me as he drops my suitcases onto the sidewalk in front of the apartment building. I follow after him, grabbing one of the handles as he slides them up. "That's different. You of all people should know that."

"Whatever," I mumble. "I didn't ask for you to do all of this."

"And you didn't have to." He smiles at me, ignoring my attitude as he heads into the building. I follow him, inhaling the fresh scent in the building. My eyes wander around the entranceway and it feels more like an expensive hotel than an apartment building as we walk toward the elevator. "What kind of a brother would I be if I didn't do this kind of stuff for my most favorite person in the world?"

The elevator dings and the doors slide open as we both walk inside, August with a smile on his face while he presses one of the numbers, and me trying to swallow my heart down as it crawls into my throat. "You must have me confused with yourself. I'm pretty sure if anyone is your favorite, it's yourself."

"Ah, there she is," he beams, pulling me in for a sideways hug as we ride the elevator up to the seventh floor. "My snarky little sister. I was afraid that our time apart would make you lose your touch of talking shit. I can see you still have it."

I push him away, both of us laughing as he distracts my mind from what I'm about to walk into. August dives into mindless conversation about how he'll take me to campus tomorrow and make sure I get a tour and everything I need for when classes start on Monday. It isn't until we're walking up to the door to their apartment that the reality of the situation comes back to me full force.

August is about to open the door, when it's pulled open by someone on the other side. It opens wide enough for us to enter, and I see *him*. He looks like I remember, only he's matured and filled out more, his body in impeccable shape from the demands of college hockey. His inky hair is still a tousled mess that falls just above his eyebrows and his ocean blue eyes shine as they meet mine.

The corners of his plump lips lift upward into a mischievous grin, showing his perfectly straight teeth, and the air leaves my lungs in a rush. My heart pounds erratically in its cage and for a moment, I'm frozen in place as I stare back at him.

Logan Knight.

The boy I've loved my entire life.

"Welcome home."

CHAPTER TWO
LOGAN

Isla's hazel eyes are wide as she stands in the doorway, staring back at me with a shocked expression on her face. She knows that August and I live together, so I'm not quite sure why she looks as surprised as she does to see me standing here. She and August are almost exact replicas of each other, they could literally pass as twins.

Her mocha-colored hair hangs down to her waist in waves. She looks just as I remembered her, yet there's something different about her. Her body has matured more, filling out the curves of her petite frame, but it's more than just physical. The way she looks at me now, not with hearts in her eyes as she once did... it's almost as if the light dimmed. Like she knows better now.

Is there someone else who occupies her thoughts and her time now?

Shut the fuck up, Logan. I want to mentally kick myself right now. What she does is none of my business. She's my best friend's little sister. The girl that I grew up protecting as if she were my own. It's Isla fucking Whitley—and just because we kissed a few times in the past, doesn't mean a damned thing now.

"Come on, Isla," August groans, bumping the back of her legs with the suitcase. "We gotta be at practice in, like, half an hour, so let's get your shit inside, please."

I reach out to Isla as she walks into the apartment. "Here, let me at least carry something." My hand brushes against hers as I wrap it around the strap of her backpack. Her lips part slightly as if she's going to argue, but she quickly moves her hand away from mine, letting me pull the pack from her without an argument.

Well, this is going to be a lot of fun.

August brushes past the two of us, grumbling something under his breath. He's been on Coach Lindsey's shit list for the past two weeks because he was late for practice more times than not. If he's not on the ice now before practice starts, Coach won't let him play. No one is a fan of that, especially when the rest of our lives ride on our college years.

Let's just say, August has been making sure that he's there *before* practice starts. And since we live together and usually drive together, that means I get to go early too.

Not that I really mind it. It's extra ice time and that shit is not free. Even having a rink at our school —we have scheduled times that we're allowed on the ice and it's not an everyday thing. If I want a chance at the NHL, I need all of the time I can get. It's always been my dream, and my mom has been working her ass off as a self-made agent to try and help get me there.

Nothing will come between me and my dreams.

"Come on," I motion for Isla to follow me. She raises an eyebrow at me, but follows behind without protesting. "Let's get you in your new room before we have to leave. And then you can have the rest of the afternoon to get settled in without having either of us here to bother you."

We walk deeper into the apartment and I give her the official tour, although it's pretty self-explanatory. The kitchen and living room look exactly as you would expect. We walk down the hallway and I show her August's bedroom on the right. We stop at the next door that's adjacent from August's on the left. "This one is your room," I pause, moving out of the way as August slides past us and heads into his room. I motion to the room on the right that is next to August's. "That one's my room, and the bathroom is at the end of the hall."

Isla tilts her head to the side, cocking an eyebrow. "Only one bathroom with three bedrooms?"

"Yeah," I smirk, brushing past her as I walk into the fully furnished bedroom and set her backpack down on the bed. Isla walks in after me, dragging along her suitcase. "You'll either have to wait your turn to use it or get used to sharing it. Just remember to lock the door if you want privacy, because it's not a guarantee that someone won't walk in there if it's unlocked."

"You're kidding, right?" She pushes the suitcase to the bed and pulls off her beanie as she drops down onto the mattress. I take a step back, stopping beneath the threshold of the door. "You know there's a thing called boundaries, right?"

Crossing my arms over my chest, I lean my shoulder against the doorjamb with a mischievous grin playing on my lips. "I always knock before entering. Can't say the same about your brother, though."

Isla sighs, her plump lips parting as she rolls her eyes. "I see he didn't mature past high school." She unzips her thick winter coat and shrugs it off before tossing it onto the end of the bed. My eyes travel along the length of her thin torso to her full breasts.

My cock twitches in my pants and I instantly feel a twinge of guilt deep in my chest. She was always supposed to be off-limits, but the temptation has always been there. Isla was the one person that I let close enough, that I could let my guard down with and tell her all of my secrets. The connection between us was never deniable, but it was something I knew neither of us could ever act on.

And even if we did share a few private moments, I never let it go any further than making out. Isla deserved more than I could give her. She deserved to be with someone that her family would approve of. I'm fairly certain her brother might strangle me if he ever found out there was something between us. He trusted me to look after her like she was my own sister. What the fuck does that say about me if I'm supposed to view her in that way, yet I'm jerking off to the thought of her in the shower at night?

"Are you okay?" Isla's voice is soft and sounds

like a melody of its own, like the classical music she was always listening to. I bring myself back to reality, my eyes focusing on hers as her warm hazel irises search mine.

"Huh? Yeah, I'm fine," I tell her dismissively. I don't have a good enough excuse for the way I momentarily got lost in my own thoughts, so I just change the subject instead. "August and I want to take you out for dinner tonight after we're done with practice. Neither of us can cook for shit and it's only right that we show you something other than the apartment."

She folds her hands in her lap, giving me a warm smile. "I appreciate it, but you guys don't have to do that. Honestly, you can just pretend I'm not even here. I don't want to disrupt your lives at all by living here." She pauses for a moment, nervously chewing on the inside of her cheek. "I didn't know I was moving in here until we pulled up."

My eyebrows pinch together. "August didn't tell you?"

Isla shakes her head in response.

That explains the shocked look on her face. Sure, she knew that we lived together, but now it makes sense. She wasn't expecting to see me today and then everything changed as soon as she got here. I need her to feel comfortable here and like this is her home too, not that she's just staying with us as a temporary thing.

"Don't ever think you're disrupting our lives by moving in with us, okay?" I tell her, my eyes staring directly into hers. "You're a part of our lives and this is your home now too."

"Logan!" August calls from his room as he sticks his head out into the hallway. "Hurry the hell up and get ready for practice. You know I can't be late."

I roll my eyes and Isla laughs quietly as I push off the doorway. "You heard the man. Can't have him being late." A smile forms on my lips and I wink at her. "Think about what you want for dinner before we get back."

I don't give Isla a chance to respond before I leave her alone in her room and slip into my own. I glance down at my sweatpants and t-shirt. I'm going to have to change everything I'm wearing once we get to the locker room, so there's no point in changing again now. Grabbing my bag from the corner of my room, I wheel it toward the door and grab one of my sticks.

August is already heading out the front door as I wheel my bag down the hall. I pause outside of her room, glancing in as she begins to unpack her stuff.

Soft classical music sounds from somewhere inside and a smile touches my lips.

I've missed her presence—everything about her. She's still the Isla I remember. The quiet girl who liked to absentmindedly doodle in notepads and listen to soft classical melodies. The one who always paid attention and watched the world going on around her. The beautiful girl who only had eyes for me.

My Isla...

Now, I just need to remember to keep my hands to myself.

CHAPTER THREE
ISLA

After unpacking all of my things and putting them where they belong, I drop back down onto the plush mattress. I'm not sure how much time has passed since Logan and August left for practice, but I'm mentally exhausted already.

I would be lying if I said I would rather live in a dorm than in their apartment, but what happens the first time Logan brings a girl home? It's not like it would be any different from high school. He had a few different girlfriends during his time there and it never made a difference.

That's just how Logan was. He couldn't be serious about anything other than hockey. He was flakey and afraid of commitment. Maybe he was right that night... I tried to give him my virginity because I was desperate and pathetic. All I wanted was for him to love me. Now, looking back at how his past relationships went, Logan was right when he said that I deserved more than him.

I wouldn't want the relationships that those other girls had with Logan. And if there's one thing that will always remain untouchable—it's our friendship. Things are better this way and that's what I need to be my driving force. My mantra and constant reminder. *We're just friends and that's all we can ever be.*

My eyes grow heavier as I settle deeper into the comfortable bed, and I eventually let them fall shut as the soft hum of classical music lulls me to sleep. It's a dreamless sleep, which is unusual for me, but today was a long day, one filled with more surprises than I had anticipated.

I'm not sure how long I'm actually asleep for, but the mattress dips on both sides of me. Since I'm half asleep, it's confusing and I think I might just be imagining things. Or maybe it was the way I was lying. But then the smell hits me and I know I'm not alone.

I shift in the bed, rolling onto my side as I slowly wake up. My brother lies on the bed next to me, smelling like a dirty hockey bag. My nose scrunches and I close my eyes, a groan falling from my mouth as I roll back in the other direction. The smell is just as strong on the other side and I peel my eyelids open, only to find Logan sitting on this side of my bed.

"Come on," I grumble, sitting up in a sleepy daze. "You two know how badly you stink right now. You couldn't at least get a shower before coming in here?"

Logan's lips curl upward, revealing his straight white teeth. His hair is damp with sweat and I want to run my fingers through it. Even though he smells like the musty smell of hockey, he still looks so goddamn good. The stench doesn't even come close to how he looks right now.

"You know that you've missed this smell."

A giggle slips from my lips, but I quickly swallow it back, scrunching up my face. "You mean the smell of sweaty balls? No thank you. It was nice not having to live with this smell."

August rolls out of my bed, hopping onto his feet. "Well, welcome back to living with hockey players, little sis. You lived your entire life with this smell, don't even act like you're not used to it."

I roll my eyes at him as he rounds the side of the

bed, standing there as Logan stays seated on the edge of the mattress. "Can the two of you just go and shower so we can get food?"

"Did you decide what you're hungry for?" Logan asks me as he rises from my bed, and August slips out of my room.

Shaking my head, I give him an apologetic smile. "I don't know what's good around here. I was thinking maybe you guys could just take me somewhere that you both like."

"Babe, you're not twenty-one yet..." His voice trails off for a moment as he tilts his head to the side. My heart skips a beat at the sound of that word coming from his mouth. It's been so long since he called me that, but he acts unaffected—like it didn't even happen. "Although, there is a sports bar nearby that has good food and an actual restaurant part."

I swallow back my heart as it attempts to climb into my throat and nod. "Sure. Anything sounds great."

Logan gives me his infamous smile. "Perfect. We'll head out as soon as we're ready."

"Okay." I smile back at him, my voice quieter than I intended. Logan's grin falters, his eyebrows drawing closer together. He hovers in my doorway for a moment, tilting his head to the side as he assesses me. I watch as his lips part slightly, as if he wants to say something, but he doesn't. Instead, he sighs, shaking his head to himself before he ducks out of my room.

I flop onto my back on the bed, the air leaving my lungs in a defeated breath. If I were smart, I would tell my brother that I want to go stay in the dorm room that I was supposed to. I hate the way Logan looks at me, because I secretly love it. The way it makes me feel, knowing I have his attention.

And it's as if every time the smallest moment happens, I'm reminded it could never happen. How am I supposed to let go of my feelings for him when he's sleeping in the room across the hall from me? We're just friends.

As if he can hear my thoughts, Logan pokes his head back through my doorway. "Hey, Isla?" His voice is soft and gentle, but his ocean blue eyes are full of torment. "Can we talk after dinner?"

My heart constricts and my breath catches in my throat. I swallow over the knives lodged in my throat as I glance over at him and nod. My trust in my actual voice is nonexistent in this moment. Logan presses his lips together and tips his head before he leaves again.

My eyes are glued to the doorway, but my mind

is running a mile per second. Whenever someone says they want to talk, it never seems to be about anything good. I have no idea what he could possibly want to talk about, but the thought alone already has my stomach doing somersaults.

This is going to be one hell of an awkward dinner.

Reluctantly, I climb out of bed and force the butterflies away from my stomach. They're not the good kind of butterflies either. They're the nervous ones that scratch away at your insides because you have no idea what is really coming for you. It's anxiety inducing and I hate it. I quickly change my clothes, changing into a pair of leggings and a loose shirt before sliding my feet into my white Converse.

I walk across the room to where a full-length mirror hangs on the closet door and give myself a once-over. My long hair hangs in soft waves around my face and I run my fingers through the strands, working out any tangles from my nap. Satisfied with the way it looks, I push it back behind my ears and look over my makeup.

It's a light natural look, with a nude shade of eyeshadow, and mascara that makes my long eyelashes look borderline fake. I walk over to my dresser and grab my makeup bag before grabbing my blush and contour. I refresh the makeup that got messed up from rubbing my face on a pillow and spritz myself with some perfume before heading out of the bedroom.

August is already dressed, wearing a clean pair of jeans and a gray sweatshirt that has the Wyncote Wolves emblem on it. His hair is still damp, hanging over his forehead as he tilts his head down to look at his phone in his lap. He taps away, not noticing me at first as I sit down at the table across from him.

I glance down the hall, seeing that the bathroom door is still closed and the light shines from the small space between the bottom of the door and the floor. The sound of the shower cuts off and I hear the glass door open and close. My mind wanders, knowing that Logan is naked in there right now.

What the hell is wrong with you, Isla? Fucking get it together.

"Earth to Isla..." August's voice grabs my attention and I quickly tear my gaze away from the hallway and look at him. He raises an eyebrow at me, but doesn't call me out. That doesn't even come close to erasing the embarrassment as the heat creeps up my neck and spreads across my cheeks. "You didn't hear a single thing that I said, did you?"

I shake my head, swallowing roughly. "Sorry, I'm just a little distracted today."

"Right," he says suspiciously, narrowing his eyes for a moment before his face relaxes. "I asked if you and Logan figured out where we're eating?"

"Oh, yeah." I pause, clearing my throat as I nervously shift my weight in my seat. "He said something about some sports bar that has a restaurant too."

August smirks, nodding as he sits back in his chair. "O'Hallarans. There's this sexy bartender that works there that I've been meaning to catch up with."

I don't hear Logan as he walks up behind me, but I can smell the faint scent of his cologne and shampoo as he enters the room. "Poppy?" Logan chuckles as he walks past both of us at the table and stops by the island in the kitchen. "I think you fucked that up last time, man."

"Fuck you," August growls at him as he gets up from his seat. "If anyone fucked it up, it was that dumb-ass chick you brought home that night I finally got Poppy to come hang out."

My body falls rigid and I so desperately want to cover my ears, but I can't draw that kind of attention to myself. I don't want to hear about Logan and another girl. My heart clenches in my chest and my lungs burn as I hold my breath.

"Bro. She was fucking trashed. I couldn't leave her at the bar and she refused to tell me her address." Logan shakes his head, rolling his eyes as he grabs his keys from the counter. "I didn't know she was going to be all over your dick."

I glance back and forth between the two of them, thoroughly confused at this point, but I let out the breath I was holding. Logan's intentions may have been different that night, but if the girl was more interested in August, it brings me a sense of relief. I need to check myself. *Logan isn't mine...*

"Yeah, well, you owe Poppy an explanation then," August informs Logan as he walks toward the front door. "Clear that shit up for me, okay?" He pauses and glances at me, still sitting at the table. "What are you doing, Isla? Let's go."

CHAPTER FOUR
LOGAN

We end up at O'Hallarans, which is where I had originally suggested going, but I didn't think August would be sending me on a secondary mission while we are here. I just wanted to come here and grab a bite to eat, maybe get a beer or two.

Instead, I'm standing here at the bar, waiting for Poppy to be done serving some of the guys on the other side while Isla and August are sitting at a table across the room from me. I slowly spin my bottle of beer on the bar top as I attempt to wait with patience.

It doesn't take Poppy but a few more minutes before she strides over to me, a frown forming on her face. "What's up, Knight?"

Most people know me by my last name, just because of my status on the hockey team. We come here a lot after games with our teammates and that's what they all call me. I don't even know if most people know what my real first name is, but I'm so used to being called Knight, I don't bother correcting anyone.

Isla is the only one who really calls me by my first name. And there's something about the way my name sounds rolling off her tongue that makes me want to taste it on her lips.

"So, I owe you an apology."

Poppy's brows draw together and she tilts her head to the side. "Um, for what exactly? Because last time I checked, we barely ever even interact, except when you're here ordering drinks."

My nostrils flare as I inhale deeply. "For the night you were hanging out with August."

Poppy purses her lips and crosses her arms over her chest as she looks past me, no doubt, her eyes landing on August as she picks him out from across the room. "If anyone owes me an apology, it's him. Who the hell invites you over to hang out and then has another girl end up on your lap?"

"Which is my fault..." my voice trails off as I take a swig of my beer. "Ella is a friend of ours and I met her and a few other people for drinks that night. She ended up getting completely shit-faced and I couldn't leave her here. She refused to tell me what room she was in, so I figured I would bring her to our apartment to sleep it off. I didn't realize you were there and I didn't realize she had a thing for August."

"Mhmm, sure." Poppy glances around the bar. "Look, I appreciate you taking the time to say something to me, but I really gotta get back to work. Just let August know that it doesn't mean shit until I hear him grovel."

I watch as she spins on her heel, a smile plastered to her face as she makes her way over to a couple that just sat down on the other side of the bar. A sigh slips from my lips and I grab my beer and head over to the table that Isla and August are sitting at.

Isla sips on her water, her eyes meeting mine as I slide into the booth next to her. I hear the sharp intake of her breath as my thigh brushes against hers, but I don't bother moving, leaving my leg pressed against hers.

"So..." August folds his arms on the table, leaning forward as he stares at me. "What did she say? Did you tell her what really happened?"

I nod. "You're still in the dog house, dude. You're going to have to talk to her and smooth things out. She wanted me to tell you the explanation doesn't mean a thing until she hears it from you." I pause, a smirk forming on my lips as I stare back at him. "And she wants you to grovel."

"Fuck," August mumbles, lifting his beer to his lips as he takes a swig. "I mean, it's not like we're together, so technically, I'm free to do whatever I want with whomever I want."

The cushion of the bench shifts and I feel Isla's leg move as she kicks August in the shin. He winces, cutting his eyes at her. "What the hell was that for?"

"Don't be such a pig, August," Isla scolds him with a look of disgust on her face. "Seriously, what the hell is wrong with you? Just because you guys aren't in a relationship doesn't mean you can't show her some respect."

"I am respectful," August argues as he lifts his gaze to our server. We all fall silent for a moment as she sets our plates in front of us on the table. August smiles at her and waits until she's gone before he continues. "I'm just saying, she's blowing this out of proportion because we aren't together."

"Is she really, though?" Isla retorts, picking up a fry from her plate as she pops it into her mouth. "If roles were reversed, how would you feel? You wouldn't be pissed off and hurt like she is right now?"

August chuckles around a mouthful of burger. I go to reach for the bottle of ketchup at the other side of the table, but Isla grabs it as she sees me moving for it. A soft smile touches her lips as she hands it to me. I wrap my hands around the bottle, my fingertips brushing against hers. She inhales deeply and a warmth spreads through my stomach as the feeling of her sets my skin on fire.

Goddamn. In an instant, it all comes rushing back. The stolen kisses and the secretive touches in her bed late at night. I missed her. And even though I know it could never be any more than what it once was, I still want to feel that again with her.

Isla quickly lets go of the ketchup and quickly recovers as she begins to eat her sandwich that she ordered. I dump some of the condiment onto my plate as August doesn't pick up on anything that just happened between us.

"She's right, August," I tell him, dipping a fry in the ketchup. "You know that if some guy came onto Poppy like that while the two of you were hanging out, you wouldn't have been happy about it."

August glances back and forth between the two

of us. "You two are supposed to be on my side, you know."

"Not when you're in the wrong," Isla retorts, smiling sweetly as she takes a sip of her water. "Either make things right with her or let the poor girl move on."

"Fine," August submits, taking a gulp of his beer. "Let me finish my burger and then I'll go talk to her."

I grab his plate, sliding it away from him and Isla's laughter makes my heart smile. "Go talk to her now, because I don't want to be here all night while you sit around at the bar staring at Poppy's ass."

"Jesus, fine." August lets out an exasperated sigh as he raises his hands in defeat. "I'll go fucking talk to her." He grabs his beer and as he's sliding out of the booth, he grabs his plate of food. "I'm taking this with me, though."

Isla and I both laugh lightly at his dumb ass as he makes his way across the room and over to the bar. I glance over at her, catching her gaze already on mine. Her cheeks instantly blush, a soft pink tint consuming them as she drops her gaze down to her plate. She grabs a handful of fries and shoves them into her mouth.

This damn girl...

I take a sip of my beer, setting it down on the

table before turning in my seat to face her. "I know that I said that I wanted to talk to you after dinner, but maybe we can talk now?"

"Um," she pauses, taking a nervous sip of her water to wash down the handful of fries she just swallowed. "Sure, I guess."

I swallow hard, my eyes bouncing back and forth between hers. She stares back at me, her hazel eyes filled with an emotion I can't pinpoint. They widen slightly and I can see a wave of fear pass through them. She's on edge right now because she doesn't know what to expect from me and I instantly feel guilty.

Over the years, I programmed her to be that way without even trying. In the past, there was never anything predictable from me. I played games with her heart—her young, fragile, teenage heart—and I fucking hate myself for doing that. That doesn't mean I didn't mean anything that happened between us, I just know what I knew then. She is off-limits and always was. It was wrong of me to ever act on my impulses with her.

I've conditioned her to not know what to expect from me and I want to change that.

"I wanted to apologize to you, for the way I left."

Her eyebrows draw close together and she tilts

her head to the side. "I don't know why you're apologizing. I didn't expect for you to be there in the morning. It was kind of the way you did things back then, Logan."

My throat constricts and her words feel like a blade to my heart. "I know, but I should have at least said goodbye, but I was too much of a coward. I knew if I saw you that morning, you would have had the power to make me stay."

Isla's lips part slightly, her chest rising and falling with shallow breaths as her eyes widen. "Logan… I would never ask you to give up your dreams."

"I know you wouldn't." I pause for a moment, mulling over my words, but I'm done holding back now. She deserves my honesty if we're going to be roommates. "I knew how I felt about you then. Just one look from you would have had me questioning my entire future."

Isla takes a gulp of her water, her throat bobbing roughly as she swallows. "We don't have to do this, Logan. I don't want to go back over the past. It is what it is."

I shake my head. "It was wrong of me. I never should have acted on my impulse and those feelings. We both know why it would have never worked."

"I know," she whispers, her voice barely audible. "Like I said... we don't have to do this, okay?"

"Just listen, please..." I stare at her, my eyes desperately searching hers. I can see the hurt in her expression and that's not what I'm trying to do here. I'm trying to save us both from the destruction that this could cause. "I wasn't a good friend to you in the past and I'd like a chance to make things right."

She stares back at me, blinking a few times. "What do you mean?"

"I want to be a better friend to you, Isla... if you'll let me."

Her eyes don't leave mine, but I watch as her expression transforms into something that resembles hope. The gold and green hues in her warm irises swirl. "You want to just be friends?"

I nod, grabbing my beer as I take a nervous sip of it. It's not what I really want, but it's the best that I can do. And if we can only be friends, I'll be the best fucking friend she's ever had.

Isla smiles and my heart stops at the sight of her.

"I would like that."

CHAPTER FIVE
ISLA

My alarm sounds from the side of my bed and I groan, rolling over as I slam my hand down on the stupid device. Today is my first day of classes and I'm not exactly thrilled about it. I've only been living here for a week and have yet to make any friends that don't play on the ice hockey team. But then again, it's really not much different from the rest of my life.

I want it to be different here, though. I don't want to just be an extension of August—like a fifth limb. I want to be my own person, with my own life and my own friends. It might sound selfish, but I sacrificed a lot in my life because of everything my parents were doing for August and for the sake of him doing something with his natural ability on the ice.

There was never really much focus on the things I was interested in or wanted to do. I missed a lot of birthday parties and sleepovers at other friends' houses because we had to travel a lot on the weekends. Since our dad used to play professionally, he was very devoted to making the same dream happen for August.

My parents attempted to get me on the ice when I was little. I knew how to skate—because what sibling of a hockey star doesn't—but it wasn't something I was passionate about. It never stuck and wasn't something I wanted to spend the rest of my life doing. My mom tried to encourage me to try different sports to see if there was something I was interested in, but there was literally nothing.

I was just the quiet kid who liked to read and sketch. I was mediocre, at best, so art was never something I attempted to pursue as more than just a hobby. Now that I'm in college and have the opportunity to explore things by myself, I plan on revisiting that.

Which is why my first class today is a clay and sculpture class. It's something I never really tried, and even though it doesn't pertain to my major in teaching, I don't even care. It's something I want to do for me—something that doesn't involve August —and I'm at the point in my life where I'm ready to be selfish.

As I slip into the hallway, the rest of the apartment is quiet and the bathroom door is open. I quickly shuffle down the hall and head into the room, shutting the door behind me. I don't bother attempting to lock it, because that was one thing Logan failed to mention, but it didn't take long for me to figure it out. They didn't lock the door in here because it was broken.

And them being them—neither made an attempt to get it fixed. They both just rolled with it and went along with life like it didn't matter. Me, on the other hand? It feels a little uncomfortable knowing someone could walk in here at any given moment. But at the same time, it's just my brother and his best friend. The one guy who I knew like the back of my hand.

I strip out of my clothes and jump into the shower, cranking the water up until it feels like it's scalding my skin. Closing my eyes, I step back, letting the hot water run over my long hair. Beads of water trickle down my face as I grab my shampoo and work a lather into my hair. August and Logan shouldn't be up for a few hours, so I take my time washing my hair and my body.

The warmth of the water wraps its arms around me like a comforting blanket. Growing up in the mountains in Vermont, our summers never felt like they were long enough. You grow accustomed to the cold over time, especially when you're born in the snow, but sometimes, there's nothing quite as comforting as the heat.

My parents always found a reason to take us on a summer vacation, somewhere away from the cold, and it was the one thing I was very fond of. I looked forward to it every year, especially after constantly feeling like a walking ice cube. We always went somewhere south—far enough away that you couldn't detect the frigid temperatures we lived in.

I should have picked a college in a warmer state. I don't know why I decided to come to Wyncote University. Maybe it had to do with the fact that my brother came here and I couldn't seem to stop following around in his shadow. Or maybe, subconsciously, it was because of Logan. I would never admit it aloud, but I would follow him anywhere that he asked me.

The door to the bathroom suddenly opens and I freeze in the hot water. I throw my arms over my chest, feeling completely exposed behind the glass door as I turn my back on the intruder. "Get out!"

I hear the sound of his chuckle and I glance over my shoulder, noticing his dark hair through the foggy glass. Fucking Logan. Of course, it's him. I'm embarrassed as hell and in a position that I don't want him to see me in.

"I just gotta take a piss and I'll leave, okay?"

"Logan," I grit his name through clenched teeth, attempting to shield my body with my hands, even though he probably can't see anything but the tone of my skin because of the condensation on the glass shower walls. "If you can't tell, I'm freaking naked right now. So, please, just go pee outside or something."

He glances over his shoulder at me and I can't make out his expression, but I hate being under his gaze right now. It sends a warmth straight to the pit of my stomach and I clench my thighs together, fighting against the shiver that runs down my spine.

"I know that you're naked in there..." His voice is hoarse and strained as if the thought alone pains him. He clears his throat and flushes the toilet before moving over to the sink. "How are you getting to class this morning?"

His question catches me off guard. "August said I

could take his car," I tell him, shifting under the water as it grows colder.

"Let me drive you," he says quietly as he leaves the sink running and dries his hands before brushing his teeth. He turns around, leaning against the counter as he faces the shower.

"You don't have to do that."

I can still feel his eyes on me as I shift and turn off the water in an attempt to get him to leave the bathroom since I finished showering minutes ago. If I don't get out of here soon, I'm going to be late to my first class. The chill from the cold air runs over my body, sending a shiver through my flesh as goosebumps erupt over my skin.

Covering my naked breasts with my arms, I turn to face him, staring at him through the condensation on the shower door. Logan pushes off the counter and grabs my towel from the hook on the wall before tossing it over the top of the door. Keeping one arm over my chest, I catch it with my other hand before it hits the wet floor beneath my feet.

In haste, I wrap it around my body, ignoring my soaking wet hair that hangs down my back. Logan moves out of the way as I push open the door and step out into the coldness of the room. I don't have time to worry about the way he's looking at me and be embarrassed by him walking in on me in the shower.

Ignoring him, I step to the counter, pulling my long hair over my shoulder as I stare into the mirror. Logan steps behind me, his eyes finding mine through the glass. "I know I don't have to drive you, but I want to." His voice is soft, his ocean blue eyes tormented as they search mine. He lingers for a moment, before turning away with a sigh of defeat. "I'll be waiting for you when you're ready to go."

I watch through the mirror as he disappears from the bathroom, pulling the door shut behind him to give me some privacy. I'm left alone with my conflicting thoughts and I'm not sure how to decipher the interaction that just happened between us.

I can't let him mess with my heart and my head again... not this time.

CHAPTER SIX
LOGAN

The ride to campus is awkwardly quiet. Isla is clearly lost in her own thoughts as she shuffles through her papers and the map of the school. I glance over at the mess on her lap as we pull up to a red light and notice that she has her entire route mapped out with a highlighter. I'm sure it has everything to do with the fact that she's anxious as shit going to a new school with people she doesn't even know.

The only two people she knows are me and August. She met a few of the guys we play hockey with, but she doesn't know them like she knows us. And she has yet to meet anyone who is actually in any of her classes. I partially feel bad for that. I should have offered to take her to try and meet people, but August said he had it all covered.

He obviously had his head too far up his ass to make an attempt to show Isla around and she was too kind to bother asking him. That's just the way Isla operated. Her parents tried to make it seem like they didn't have favorites when it came to their children, but Isla was always the one who just went with the flow.

She acted as if it didn't affect her that she spent all of her free time being consumed by her brother and hockey. And because of that, her parents didn't really see how unfair it was on her, how she missed out on so much with her friends and other girls her age. Isla never wanted to rock the boat or upset anyone, even if it was at the expense of her own happiness.

And now I feel like a goddamn asshole, driving her to campus only to drop her off. It's no different than what she's been used to her entire life and for the first time in a long time, I really want to just punch her damn brother square in the face.

Instead of pulling up to the front of the campus, I pull my car into the parking lot and find a space as close to the front as I can. Isla quickly shoves her stuff back into her bag, except for the highlighted map she has. She glances over at me, perplexed and worried as I put the car in park.

"Thanks for the ride," she says softly, a smile touching her lips as she throws her backpack over her shoulder. "You really didn't have to, but I appreciate you doing this. I'm still not familiar with the roads around here, so it was nice to not have to worry about getting lost."

"I told you that I wanted to drive you and I meant it. I don't like the thought of you trying to figure all of this out in a new place with new people by yourself."

Isla reaches for the door handle, a pink tint spreading across her cheeks as she diverts her gaze from my eyes. "Well, I really appreciate it, Logan. Thank you."

She climbs out of the car, softly shutting the door behind her as I kill the engine and reach for my own door handle. I watch her as she begins to walk away from me, without even noticing as I get out and begin to walk after her.

"Isla, wait up!" I call after her, extending my stride to shorten the distance between us.

Isla stops, spinning on her heel with her eyes wide in surprise. "What are you doing? I thought you were just dropping me off?"

My brows draw together as I tilt my head to the side. "Why would I bother parking in the parking lot? If I were dropping you off, I would have pulled up out front."

She shifts her weight nervously on her feet, adjusting her strap on her shoulder as she gives me a shy smile and shrugs. "I don't know. I just thought that maybe you didn't want anyone to see you dropping me off out front or something."

What the fuck?

I stare at her, losing myself in the gold and green hues that swirl in her irises. My heart crawls into my throat and I feel uncomfortable with her admission. She thought I would make her walk across the damn parking lot because I didn't want anyone to see her getting out of my car? I couldn't care less what anyone thinks and it leaves me speechless—her thinking I could possibly be embarrassed by being seen with her. I wanted to keep what we had hidden, not her. Never her.

"Give me the map," I tell her, my hand reaching out as I close the distance between us. Isla's eyes bounce back and forth between mine as she hesitates, but with reluctance, she hands it over to me.

I scan the paper, taking note of her classes and the rooms jotted down in her curly handwriting on the side. Each is labeled with the times and colored with the same highlighter that marks the map in order of her classes. A smile touches my lips when I see her first class.

"Clay and sculpture?" I ask her, raising an eyebrow as my lips curve. I've seen Isla's artistic abilities and they are something to be envious of. But it was something that was all self-taught because she didn't want to bother her parents with taking an interest in one of her hobbies. That was the fucking selfless Isla I've always known. "I like it."

Isla peers up at me through her dark lashes with a small smile. "Art was always something that I enjoyed and since I have some electives that I can take, I figured I'd try some different art classes even though it isn't my major."

I glance up at the front of the school, noticing the crowd of students is slowly thinning out. The massive clock built into the brick tower shows we literally have five minutes to get her to her class that is on the other side of the building and we're only halfway through the parking lot.

Reaching for her hand, I grab it, lacing my fingers through hers without even thinking about it as I pull her along with me. She stumbles slightly but recovers quickly as she follows along after me, her legs moving faster to keep up with my stride.

"I've seen what you can do with art." I tell her, glancing down at her as she walks along beside me. Her hand feels so right in mine, but reality quickly catches up to me and I drop it, without seeming too obvious as I grab my phone from my pocket and pretend to check it before sliding it back into my pocket. "Why isn't that your major?"

Isla slides her arm through the other strap of her backpack and clutches them with both hands so I can't touch her again. She gives me an incredulously look as harsh laughter spills from her lips. "Are you kidding? My parents are supportive, but I don't know if they're that supportive…" She pauses, shaking her head as she sighs. "Art doesn't pay the bills and since I don't have hockey to fall back on, I need to get a degree in a field that is actually going to let me be self-reliant."

I stop for a moment, grabbing her shoulder to pull her to a halt as she continues to walk past me. Isla turns around to face me, but I don't move my hand. "Don't discredit yourself, Isla. Don't you dare give up on your dreams. You deserve to do whatever is going to make you happy and I've seen your artwork. I believe in you."

She stares at me for a moment, her expression soft and her eyes growing wet, like this is something that no one has ever said to her. Does no one else believe in this fucking girl? She might not be August Whitley—hockey superstar—but that doesn't mean a damn thing. She's Isla fucking Whitley and she can do anything she puts her mind to.

"Thank you." Her voice is so soft, it's barely audible, but the sound snakes its way around my eardrum. "I really do have to get to class, though, or I'm going to be late."

"No shit," I laugh lightly, spinning her back around before giving her a small shove. "That's exactly why I'm walking you to class, because your ass is definitely going to get lost."

"Hey," she growls, glaring at me as she bites back her smile. "I'm not that bad with directions."

I roll my eyes at her, chuckling softly as we reach the front door to the main building. "Says the girl who got lost driving to the gas station that's two blocks from our apartment."

"That's not even fair!" She lightly shoves her hand against my shoulder before walking in through the door as I hold it open for her. "I'm new here, okay?"

"Babe... the gas station is only two blocks away..."

I swallow hard, my heart pounding erratically as soon as the word leaves my lips. Isla's eyes widen slightly but she quickly brushes it away from her expression, her smile falling neutral. "Whatever," she mumbles, shaking her head in frustration. "If you can get me to my first class, I'm going to prove you wrong and won't get lost going to any of my other classes."

"Aw man. And here, I cleared my whole schedule today to make sure I could get you to every room safely," I joke, a smirk falling on my lips as we walk through the halls, walking closer to the art wing. "Are you saying that you don't need me?"

We reach the room and she pauses outside of the door as I pull it open for her, flashing me a bright smile. "Nope," she says with a wink before disappearing into the classroom without another word.

I let the door shut, staring after her through the small glass pane as she moves farther into the classroom and finds a seat at one of the tables. A chuckle rumbles in my chest and I shake my head with a smirk still playing on my lips.

She might not need me, but I need her...

CHAPTER SEVEN
ISLA

The first two weeks of school have gone by in a blur. It's been hectic, trying to settle into a routine, especially being in a new place with new people. August and Logan have both been busy with getting back into the swing of things with their demanding hockey schedule, on top of trying to maintain their school work.

We've all been seeing each other more in passing and settling down to watch a movie some evenings before they both inevitably fall asleep on the couch before the movie even finishes. They started having practice early in the morning, so they've practically turned into old men, falling asleep super early.

I'm not complaining. I know how their lives are and I don't want them to feel like they have to entertain me since I'm August's little sister that they decided to move into their apartment. Plus, I want this to be my own experience, too, and not be following them around like a lost puppy. Which is why I'm so glad I met Octavia.

She's a freshman as well and moved from Michigan for their art program here. I met her my first day, in clay and sculpture, and it turned out that we actually had a lot of classes together. We hit it off pretty quickly and it was nice to feel like I have a friend to call my own. Someone who is just as lost as I am, but yet we still have enough in common that we don't struggle to come up with conversation.

Her story is a little different than mine, since she didn't follow her brother and her childhood crush here. She's an only child who wanted to get away from her hometown. I can't say I blame her for that either, though. Octavia got to know a few other kids here before I did and she didn't even hesitate to introduce me to her group of friends who took me in like I belong with them.

It's a Friday and I'm so thankful that the weekend is beginning in about thirty minutes. A week packed full of classes gets a little tiring. Octavia told me about a party at the frat house our friend Silas was invited to. I wasn't much for partying, but it was going to be my first time at a college house party and I wasn't about to pass that up.

Our professor stands from her desk, going over our assignment that is due on Monday, before dismissing us. Octavia and I both rise from our seats and shove our things into our bags before shuffling out of the classroom after the other students. When we reach the hall, Silas is already standing out there, waiting with Demi.

"Hey, girls!" Demi says, showing her bright white teeth as she pushes her long blonde hair back over her shoulders. She and Silas walk over to us, giving us each a quick hug. "You guys ready for tonight?"

"Hell yes," Octavia sighs, adjusting her bag on her shoulder. "I need something to take my mind off the fact that I haven't even started this damn assignment that's due on Monday."

"Sunday, we're spending the day in the library until we both finish this shit," I tell her, feeling the same pressure. I had already started mine, but essays weren't exactly my forte. If it were something that involved sketching or sculpting, it would be a completely different story. Written words aren't my strongest suit.

"Enough of this," Silas interjects, wrapping his

arm around the top of Demi's shoulders. "No more talking about school shit. We're going to this party and we're getting hammered tonight, got it?"

Demi laughs. "Oh, hell yes. I need to get, like, blackout drunk tonight."

Octavia links her arm in mine as we all start walking down the hall together. "Did you wanna come meet us here and we can all walk there? It's only two blocks away and you can crash in my room tonight so you don't have to worry about getting a ride home."

"That works," I smile at her, releasing her arm as we all file through the door out to the front of the school. "Can I just leave my bag in your room before we leave then?"

"Of course," she says, her smile reaching mine. We all pause out front as we reach the main courtyard and a black BMW pulls up out front. My heart crawls into my throat as I know exactly who it is sitting behind the wheel. August had been letting me use his car since they started their early morning practices, so I wasn't anticipating a ride home today.

Silas raises an eyebrow and glances at me as the passenger's side window slides down. "Who's that?"

Demi looks over at him. "You seriously don't

know who that is?" She pauses, shaking her head. "That's Logan Knight. He's only, like, one of the star hockey players... not to mention a total fucking god. Have you never seen him before, Silas?"

"Trust me, I've seen him and the way that every girl looks at him. What I wouldn't give to look like that... Jesus." Silas pauses, rolling his eyes. "I swear, he and August get all of the girls' attention."

Octavia elbows him in the ribs. "Don't be a fucking asshole. August is Isla's brother and she lives with him and Logan." She glances over at me, giving me a sympathetic smile. "Sorry. I think sometimes Silas's dick gets a little jealous of the pussy he doesn't get."

I swallow hard over the lump in my throat and flash a fake-ass smile. I have yet to see Logan bring a girl home and I've heard Poppy's voice a few times, late at night when everyone's in bed already. Now that I think of it, though, just because I've never seen Logan bring a girl home, doesn't necessarily mean anything. That doesn't mean he doesn't have someone else's attention and that they don't have his.

It would make sense with how distant he's been toward me...

"I'll see you guys later tonight," I tell my friends

who are caught in an argument as I push past them. "Or, I'll call you when I'm getting ready to head over."

"Sounds good, girl!"

I stride over to the side of Logan's car, bending down as I reach the window and stare inside at him. His sunglasses cover his deep blue eyes, but I can feel them burning holes through mine as I stare at him. "What are you doing here?"

"Taking you home."

My eyebrows pinch together. "I drove August's car this morning. I can't just leave it here."

Logan pulls his sunglasses down the bridge of his nose as he stares back at me, his lips tipping upward. "He already got it."

I narrow my eyes at him. "So, unless I want to walk or pay for an Uber, I'm supposed to ride back with you?"

"Why are you making such a big deal about it?" Logan's smile falls and he looks at me with a touch of irritation and confusion. He directs his gaze past me, his eyes narrowing on my group of friends who are still standing back there. "You don't want your new little friend seeing you getting in another guy's car?"

I glance over my shoulder, catching Silas's eyes

on the two of us. Turning my head, I look back at Logan and raise an eyebrow. "Why the hell would I care what he thinks? He's literally just a friend."

"Mhm," Logan murmurs, rolling his eyes. "No guy is ever just friends with a girl. There's always something lingering below the surface and I saw the way he was watching you. It's only a matter of time before he acts on it."

My heart pounds erratically in my chest as my breath catches in my throat. *No guy is ever just friends with a girl.* That's exactly what Logan is supposed to be—my friend. I can't let my mind get wrapped around his words because I'm sure there's no hidden meaning behind them. He couldn't possibly mean us too, or he would have acted on it before.

Instead, I decide to toy with him. "It sounds like you're jealous, Knight."

He narrows his eyes at me. "I know how fucking college guys are, Isla. Now, get in the damn car."

Pushing off the side of the car, I cross my arms over my chest in defiance. "And what if I don't?"

Logan lets out an exasperated sigh, a shadow passing over his expression. "I won't hesitate to pick you up and toss you in here."

A smile breaks out across my face and I drop my arms to my sides before pulling open the car door.

Logan's eyes are still on mine and I can't quite read his expression as he watches me carefully. "Don't get all alpha on me. I was planning on getting in anyways, I just wanted to see your reaction."

"Don't test me, babe," he says, his voice low as he puts the car in drive and eases it away from the curb. He falls silent, keeping his eyes trained on the road as he leaves campus and heads back toward the apartment. I swallow roughly over the nervousness that builds in my throat. His reaction throws me off. I've never seen Logan act like this before and I'd be lying if I said that it didn't excite me.

I like seeing him jealous. I like the facade of hope that maybe he does feel something too…

CHAPTER EIGHT
LOGAN

Fucking Isla.

I wish I could be honest with her, but I know I can't. There's too much at stake and I don't know that it would be worth the risk. The last thing I want to do is ruin her life, especially when I know she deserves better than me. Not only that, but I'm pretty positive I would lose my best friend in the process.

My skates slide across the ice, kicking up pieces as I stop directly in front of the puck. Lifting my arms up, I hold my stick back and bring it down with such force as my slap shot connects with it, sending the puck hurling through the air.

It slices through the air, my chest and shoulders

heaving with deep breaths as I watch it enter the top corner pocket of the net.

"You good, bro?" August asks as he skates up next to me. "You working out some shit with all the fucking slap shots you've been hitting tonight?"

We had practice this morning, but Coach said the rink would be open tonight if we wanted to get some extra ice time in. I play the position more of the enforcer. I'm the one who fucks shit up and mainly gets assists. August plays center, so if anyone should be working on shots, it should be him.

Thankfully, all of the other guys cut out earlier, so I'm not sending pucks flying at our goalie before our first game this weekend. The last thing that I want to do is take the aggression out on him, but fuck, I need some kind of an outlet after taking Isla home this afternoon. That fucking girl is going to destroy me without even realizing it.

"It's just been a week," I tell August, as I skate backward away from him. "I'm saving my energy to check the shit out of the team we're playing tomorrow."

August nods, giving me a knowing look as he skates past me, pulling the puck from the net with his stick. "You wanna get this shit put away so we can head back. There's a party at the frat house tonight that I wanted to go check out if you're game?"

I skate over to the net, pulling it away as I slide it across the ice to the end of the rink. August slides across the ice, collecting the other pucks. Going to a party when we have a game tomorrow afternoon probably isn't the best decision, but I could have a beer or two and just not get wasted and be okay.

Skating over to August, I help him get the pucks off the ice. "I think that Isla went with some of her friends, so I kind of want to make sure she's okay. You know how those parties can get."

My stomach sinks and my jaw clenches as I skate to the other end of the rink and grab the other net before pushing it off the ice. I don't fucking like it, and the thought of Isla being at a frat party makes my blood boil. Half of the guys there are pigs and she's fresh meat. She's an easy target, with how goddamn innocent and kind she is. Not to mention the fact that she looks like she was sent here from heaven.

There's no way in hell I'm not going to that party now.

Pushing off on my skates, I speed over to August, feeling the burn in my legs as my blades slice through the ice. August is already off the rink and I don't stop, hopping out onto the walkway as I reach the gap in the boards. "I'm in."

We both showered in the locker rooms and changed into our clothes that we wore to the rink before heading out. Coach said that he was coming later to close things up, so we cleaned up as best we could to make his job a little easier.

As bad as it sounds, the only thing on my mind right now is getting to that party and making sure that Isla is good. I know August is concerned about his little sister being in a place with new people. Her first college party. But concerned doesn't even begin to touch how I'm feeling.

Possessive. Protective. Fucking jealous as hell thinking about her there with her douchebag friend that she made.

I saw the way he was looking at her, his eyes trained on her ass when she bent down to lean on the side of my car to talk to me. He can tell her that they're just friends, but I know better. I know how someone can feel about Isla because I've felt it for years. She deserves better than I would ever be able to give her, but he's not it.

I'll be the one to decide who is good enough or not for her.

I'm able to find a parking spot about a block away from the party but not any closer because the streets are packed with cars. Most of the kids probably walked from campus, but there are a good amount that live in their own apartments and stuff too, so I'm sure some of the cars belong to other students.

August and I both make our way down the street and when we reach the house, the entire place is lit up. It's like something out of a movie, with the front yard littered with people drinking from red Solo cups. The front door hangs wide open, all of the windows are propped open and you can feel the bass from the music playing inside while standing outside of the damn building.

I glance around the front yard, seeing some of the guys from our team and some different people from our classes. My greetings are short-lived, while August hangs around for a moment, catching up with them like he didn't just see some of them earlier today. I don't have time for mundane conversations.

I need to find Isla.

As I scan the yard, I don't see her or her friends

standing anywhere. August walks over to me after breaking away from the group of people that he was talking to. He raises an eyebrow at me and I shrug, not having anything to tell him, but I don't bother hanging around as I push through the crowd of people gathered on the front porch and head inside the house.

It's like a damn ocean filled with people as they all move around the house. The first room is packed with people just standing around and talking, along with a beer pong table set up on the other side of the room. August waves to some of them, stopping at the keg to grab himself a beer as I continue through the house. My eyes travel through the rooms as my feet move me along, looking for any sign of her, but I don't see her anywhere.

I make my way through a living room, glancing around at the couches and chairs, but I still don't see Isla anywhere. Where the hell could this girl be? After a lap around the entire first floor, searching every room high and low, the pit of my stomach rolls with dread as I realize she's nowhere to be seen down here.

This could mean one of two things. She's either upstairs with someone or outside.

Fuck.

I should just let August handle this. She is his little sister and when it comes down to it, she isn't my responsibility. If there's anyone here who should be looking for her, it should be him, but instead I catch sight of him talking to some chick from our chemistry class as he sips his beer. So much for him and Poppy being a possible thing.

This is how August operates, though. He doesn't form any real attachments because he couldn't commit if he wanted to. He's got an issue and a phobia of it. The only thing he fully commits to is hockey and I can't blame him for that. People in life will lie and leave. They'll leave you without hesitation and never reach out again—just like my own fucking dad. Hockey is one thing that will never leave... it will never let you down.

Stopping by the keg, I grab a plastic cup and fill it to the brim with the frothy beer and chug it. I glance up at the stairs, noticing some people standing in the stairwell, a few of them with their mouths fused together. I refill my cup and drain half of it before heading in the direction of the steps with my blood already boiling.

My footsteps are heavy but quick as I stride up the stairs, skipping every other step. I don't bother paying attention to the couples that I pass on the way, with only one thing on my mind. I stop at the first door that is closed and push it open without bothering to knock. A dude and some chick are half naked on the bed, yelling at me to get the fuck out as I stand there for a moment.

Backing out, I pull the door shut and turn down the hall to the next door. The next three are the same, with couples in there fucking around, and none of them involve Isla. I turn down one of them who invites me to join in. I'm not judging anyone who's into that, but I only have my sights set on her right now.

The last door that I find is locked. My stomach sinks and my heart crawls into my throat. Curling my fists, I pound on the slab of wood until it sounds like it's about to crack under the force. It's suddenly ripped open in front of me and the guy on the other side is in my face, practically screaming at me. I look past him, not finding Isla in there, and let out a breath of relief before turning away from them.

Thank fuck she wasn't in any of these rooms. So, that can only mean she's outside…

And I'm not so sure I'm going to like what I find out there any more than what I would have found up here.

CHAPTER NINE
ISLA

"Yo, Isla," Octavia calls out my name as she stumbles toward me with Demi. "You wanna hit this joint?"

I glance up at the two of them from the bench seat I'm sitting on and shake my head. "No, I'm good. I don't really smoke weed."

"Aww come on," Demi throws her arm around Octavia's shoulders, slurring her words with how sloppy drunk she already is. "A little bit of weed never hurt anyone. Plus, this is your first college party!"

Octavia grabs the joint from Demi as she waves it in my face, attempting to pressure me. "Let it go, Dem, she said no. Don't be a bitch about it."

Demi opens her mouth to say something, but then the song switches to something more upbeat through the speakers and she breaks out into a huge grin. "Oh my god, I love this song," she yells out, pulling Octavia with her. "Let's go dance!"

Octavia glances over her shoulder at me. "You coming, Isla?"

I shake my head, smiling back at her as I slowly sip my beer. It's my fifth one of the night and I'm already starting to feel warm and fuzzy. Definitely tipsy. The last thing that I need to do right now is attempt to stand up. I've been to high school parties and have had my fair share of drunken nights, but it's been a while since I've drank alcohol. And I can't remember the last time I was drunk like this.

Sitting on the piece of lawn furniture, my eyes scan the patio area, watching everyone as they're engaging in different conversations. There's two beer pong tables set up and one with flip cup. It's a chilly evening, but it's still warm enough to be outside with a sweatshirt on. And the alcohol definitely helps with the chill in the air.

I don't know any of the people here and even though I was introduced to some earlier, I've already forgotten their names. Remembering something like that has always been difficult for me, unless someone has a definitive impact on my life or makes their place known in my circle of friends. I've always been an introvert, so this is definitely out of my comfort zone—being here with a crowd of people that I don't really know.

Hence, why I'm sitting here on the bench by myself. The circle of friends I've made the past two weeks at school are small and I'm perfectly okay with that. I'm just as content, sitting here drunk as hell, people watching like it's no one's business. It has always interested me, studying people and the way they interact.

And wondering why the hell I can't do the same. It's almost like they're the replicas of how I wish I could be, interacting with people. They make it seem so easy, but every time I try to talk to someone I don't know, I struggle with the small talk. Give me one-on-one conversation, something deep and with meaning and I'm more than good.

The cushion that I'm sitting on shifts and I glance over as Silas drops down beside me. His eyes are bloodshot and glazed over as he gives me a lopsided grin. "What are you doing, sitting over here by yourself? I thought I would have found you inside dancing with the girls."

I shrug, taking another sip of my beer. "That's

not really my scene. I'm more content just hanging out here."

"I get that," he says with understanding as he pulls out a pack of cigarettes and lights one. I stare at the side of his face as he watches a group of guys playing flip cup. Silas is one of the only guys I've become friends with since my freshman year started and I like the friendship we've fallen into. He's easy to talk to and even though he's single, he's never made me feel uncomfortable.

"Why aren't you in there with them or playing beer pong or something?" I question him, my eyes trailing along the straight lines of his face. Silas is attractive, with his perfectly symmetrical face and deep green eyes. His olive skin stands out from his darker features and his dark brown hair is always perfectly styled. "I'm sure you don't want to spend your night sitting here with a wet towel."

Silas tilts his head back, laughing as a cloud of smoke curls into the night sky. He looks over at me, his green eyes finding mine. "You're not a wet towel, Isla." He smiles, chuckling lightly before his face falls serious. "This is exactly where I want to be right now."

He inches closer, sliding across the cushion as

his thigh rests against mine. Moving his cigarette to his other hand, he wraps his arm around the tops of my shoulders. The feeling is foreign, but it feels nice, tucked against his side. Silas is warm and it's getting colder as the night grows longer. "Is this okay?" he asks, peering down at me.

My heart thrums harder in my chest and I nod slowly. I appreciate his respect for boundaries and the way he asks for consent for something so simple. I've never thought of him as more than a friend—and maybe it's the alcohol—but right now, it feels nice being close to him.

"Get your fucking arm off her."

Inhaling sharply, my breath gets caught in my throat as the sound of Logan's voice sends a shiver down my spine. I glance behind the bench we're sitting on and see him standing there, his expression dark as he glares at the two of us.

Silas ignores him, taking another drag of his cigarette. Neither of us move and I'm frozen in place, unable to tear my gaze away from Logan's. He looks like he's fucking livid right now and I don't miss the way his hands curl into fists as he begins to walk around to the front of us.

"You have two options, asshole." His voice is

low, his tone harsh as he pins his gaze on Silas's and rips the cigarette from his fingers and tosses it onto the ground. "Either you remove your arm from her shoulders or I remove it from your fucking body."

"Ah... Logan fucking Knight." Silas pauses, a harsh laugh falling from his lips. "How rich is this? I should have expected you to swoop in and pull some shit like this. This is what you and August always do, isn't it?"

Logan narrows his eyes at Silas while he cracks his knuckles. "Now."

"Fuck," Silas mutters as he pulls his arm away and glances at me. "You're cool with this?"

I swallow hard over the knives in my throat, feeling completely uncomfortable as my head swims from the alcohol. "It's okay." I nod at Silas. "Just go."

I stare up at Logan, not bothering to pay attention to the shit that Silas mutters as he gets up and stalks away. I'm speechless and still frozen in place. Even though I'm tipsy, the way that Logan just acted completely surprised me. It threw me off guard, just like he did in the car when he made the comment about Silas watching me getting into Logan's car.

And I don't like feeling like I'm being pissed on like I'm someone's property. There's nothing between Logan and I. He made that crystal clear when I moved in with them. So, he has no right acting like this. I'm an adult now and I don't need him to look after me like he did when we were kids.

Grabbing the side of the bench, I rise on unsteady feet and shove past Logan as I stumble away from him. I don't get far before I feel his large hand wrapping around my bicep as he hauls me back toward him. "What the fuck, Isla?"

"Seriously, Logan? I should be asking you the same question." I spin on my heel, shaking free from his grasp as I tilt my head up to look at him. He has a good foot on me in height, but my eyes meet his as I glare at him. "What the fuck was that? I don't need you to keep an eye on me, okay? I can handle myself."

"Bullshit," he mutters, shaking his head as a shadow passes over his expression. "You're drunk as shit and if I wouldn't have showed up, he would have definitely been taking you upstairs to one of the bedrooms."

My eyebrows pinch together. "And that's any of your business because…? Last time I checked, you aren't in charge of me, Logan. What I do, does not concern you."

Logan closes the space between us, his hands finding the tops of my shoulders as his eyes bounce back and forth between mine. "That's where you're wrong, babe." His voice is low, soft and warm, just like his palms on me. "Everything you do will always concern me."

My hands find his chest and I attempt to shove him away from me, but it's a feeble attempt with how solid he is. Instead, I stumble backward and his hands fall away from my shoulders. "No. You don't get to do this to me."

"Do what?" he asks, stepping back into my space. His expression softens and his gaze burns through mine. "Care about you? Make sure you're safe?"

"Is this how you treat your friends? You practically piss on them like a goddamn dog marking its territory?"

A soft chuckle falls from his lips and he raises an eyebrow at me. "My dick has been in my pants all night, Isla."

My breath catches in my throat and I quickly lift my beer to my lips, swallowing the rest of what is in the bottle in an effort to clear the lump that situated itself there. He's my brother's best friend. He's my friend. A warmth spreads through the pit of my stomach and I know it's from more than just the alcohol. *Stop thinking about his dick.*

Logan's warm fingers brush against mine as he wraps them around the neck of the bottle and takes it from me. "I think you've had enough to drink tonight."

"You're not my keeper, Knight." I glare up at him, feeling my body sway on unsteady legs. "You don't get to tell me what I can and can't do."

Logan's face falls and he tilts his head to the side with a pained look in his eyes. "Don't do that," he whispers, his voice strained.

My eyebrows pinch together. "Do what?"

"Don't call me Knight, like everyone else."

"Your friends call you Knight." I roll my eyes in a dramatic fashion before pushing past him. "I'm just making sure that I'm playing the part right."

I leave Logan outside on the patio as I march back into the house, pushing my way through a sea of people. I don't have time for these games with him. He wants to be friends, then he needs to act like my friend instead of some jealous and possessive boyfriend. Maybe there could be something between Silas and I, but how am I supposed to ever know if he just insists on inserting himself in places that he doesn't belong?

As I make my way through the crowd of people, I finally reach the hallway that leads to the front door.

Just as I turn the corner, I feel a set of hands grabbing my waist. I gasp in shock as I'm spun around and find Logan in my face, pushing me backward. He pushes me back through a door into the laundry room.

"What are you doing?" I ask him, my voice hoarse as he corners me. My back hits the wall as he plants his palms on either side of my head, caging me in. My tongue darts out to lick my lips as I stare into the depths of his ocean eyes. "Logan…"

"I don't know how to be your friend, Isla." He moves one hand from the wall, sliding it along the side of my face as he cups my cheek. His thumb is soft as he strokes my skin. "What if I don't want you to play the part anymore?"

My breath catches in my throat as my heart pounds erratically in its cage, threatening to burst from my chest at any given moment. I drop my eyes to his plump lips before looking back into his eyes. "You don't want to be friends?"

A ghost of a smile plays on his lips as he shakes his head. "I never wanted to be your friend."

Logan slides his hand around the back of my neck as his mouth crashes into mine. His lips are warm and soft against mine, just as I remember him. It's like we're thrust back in time, to a different place, a different moment—but we're not. We're not in high school, sneaking touches and kisses when no one's looking.

This isn't just a dream or a memory…

This is really happening.

CHAPTER TEN
LOGAN

In the back of my mind, I know I shouldn't be doing this with her. I was the one who proposed the idea of being friends and told her that I wanted to be a better friend to her than I was before. Yet here I am, pressing her against the wall with my lips melting against hers.

The memory of her lips was cemented in my brain and the way she kisses me is just as I remember her. Soft and tender, sweet and innocent. Isla was always the one thing that was consistent in my life and feeling her this close again makes me regret ever missing a moment with her.

Opening my lips, my tongue darts out and I trace the seam of her lips before she parts them and lets me in. She tastes like alcohol and candy as my tongue tangles with hers, deepening the kiss as I breathe her in. I've missed her so badly that it fucking hurts in ways I could never put into words. She breaks my heart in two, just feeling her in such a close proximity.

Isla lifts her arms, wrapping them around the back of my neck as I press my body against hers, feeling her warmth. With one hand holding her in place, I slide the other down to her thin waist, grabbing her hip. She's matured since the last time I've felt her this close and fuck, I could come apart right now.

She kisses me back, her mouth moving in tandem with mine and we get lost in the moment, our surroundings fading. I didn't even bother to shut the door behind us, which I probably should have because I know August is lurking around here somewhere. I don't even care at this point. Let him fucking find us. Let this all go up in flames.

At least I'll burn, knowing I had one last taste of her before it all went to hell.

Finally breaking apart, we both come up for air as I press my forehead against hers. Both of our breathing is shallow and ragged and her warm breath skates across my face. Closing my eyes, I savor the moment, feeling her again.

"Can I ask you something?" she whispers, her voice barely audible over the music that pounds through the speakers throughout the house.

I pull away from her, my eyes meeting hers. "You can always ask me anything."

"You don't have a girlfriend or anything, do you?" She pauses for a moment, pulling her bottom lip between her teeth as she clamps down. "I don't want to be the girl who ruins a relationship or anything."

A soft chuckle falls from my lips. "No, I don't have a girlfriend. I'm not seeing or talking to anyone." I move my hand to cup the side of her face. "I haven't had a girlfriend since high school. I'm not going to lie to you and tell you that I haven't done anything with anyone since I've been here, but it's never been anything serious. As hard as I've tried, I've never been able to get you out of my head."

She stares up at me, frowning, which confuses me. "You told me that I deserved better than you, so why would you waste your time being stuck on me?"

"Because even though I don't deserve you, that doesn't mean there's anyone who comes close to you. I refuse to settle for anything less than greatness, baby. And that's exactly what you are."

I drop my hand from her face, pulling her flush

against me as she rests her head against my chest. Wrapping my arms around her waist, I hold her close as I bury my face in the crook of her neck, inhaling her sweet scent that is imprinted in my mind.

"Why do you sell yourself short?" she asks quietly, holding on to me as her legs grow tired. "You exude confidence, yet you don't see yourself the way you make others see you. It's like you only see yourself in a negative light and I disagree with everything you say about yourself, Logan. You're the best person I know."

This girl melts my heart with her sweetness, just like she always has. She's quiet, constantly observing the world around her. She can read people like no one I've ever met, always able to sympathize and make someone feel as if they are someone. Like they're important and actually mean something. She has a gift with people, one that I would never be able to obtain.

"Your brother is my best friend," I remind her quietly as I try to not kill the mood between us. "He knows all of my secrets and shortcomings. Do you really think he would approve if he knew about this?"

"I don't know," she says softly, her voice somber.

"But I know August would support whatever makes me happy. And if he knew the truth, I don't think he would be as against it as you think he would."

I don't know that I fully agree with her. It's hard to say how he would react. If I were in his shoes, I would never approve. She might not see me the same way that I see myself, but this is still a risky edge to be toeing. Before this goes any further, we both need to make sure that we're ready to jump off the cliff, regardless of what the consequences might be.

Isla sways in my arms and I can feel her body growing heavier as we stand here together. "Let's get you home, baby."

"Mmm," she murmurs against my chest. "I would like that. I definitely think I need to go to sleep."

Turning her, I slide my arm around her back as I loop the other under her knees and lift her into my arms. She groans slightly, her head rolling before she regains control of it. "You know, I can walk."

"Are you sure about that?" I ask her, chuckling softly as she leans her head against my chest and sighs. "You didn't seem too steady on your feet, so let me carry the weight for you."

"Okay," she whispers, wrapping her arms around the back of my neck. "Thank you, Logan."

A smile touches my lips but I don't respond to her as she settles into my arms and I carry her out of the laundry room. Tonight didn't go exactly how I had imagined it would, but life has a funny way of just letting things happen. I don't know what we're really doing here, but for now, this is enough.

I carry her through the house, inching closer to the door, when I catch August's eyes through the doorway that leads into the living room. His eyebrows draw together when he sees Isla in my arms and he pushes through the crowd as he rushes over to us.

"What's going on?" he questions me, his eyes scanning Isla with a worried look passing through them. "Is she okay?"

"She's fine," I tell him, pausing as she adjusts slightly in my arms. "She just had a little too much to drink so I was going to take her back to the apartment."

A sigh of relief escapes August and the worried expression leaves his face as he glances back into the living room. "I'll head home with you guys too."

I shake my head. "I got it, bro. You just stay here and enjoy yourself. Our game isn't until tomorrow evening, so it's not like we have to get up early or anything. You deserve to have some fun tonight."

August looks at Isla before looking back at me. "Are you sure?"

"Of course," I nod, smiling at him. When I get her home, she's not sleeping alone and I don't really want August to be there when I climb into bed with her. It's always easier to ask for forgiveness than it is for permission. I'll deal with him in the morning after he will most likely find us together in bed. "You good to get a ride home tonight then?"

A smirk forms on August's lips as he directs his attention back into the living room where there's a large crowd dancing. I can't see who his eyes are on, but judging by the look on his face, I'm positive he has his sights set on someone tonight. "Don't worry about me," he tells me, looking back at me with a wink. "I might end up crashing somewhere else tonight, anyways."

Relief floods me and the thought of having to talk to him when he finds us in the morning vanishes. August finding some chick to dick down tonight and sleep at her place makes this so much easier—not nearly as risky. Even though Isla is drunk and needs to sleep it off, it gives us a chance to be alone without having to worry about him.

"Make sure you wrap it up," I laugh, shaking my head as I walk around him, carrying Isla to the front door. The last thing we need is for August to go and get some chick pregnant right now. Talk about a fucking curveball.

I hear August's laughter over the sound of the music as we exit the house. I carry Isla through the crowd that's gathered on the lawn and make my way down the street to my car. Isla's eyes open as we reach the passenger's side and I let her down onto her feet as she leans against the car while I open the door. After helping her inside, I softly close the door and get in the driver's side, slipping in behind the wheel.

Isla leans her head against the cool window as I start the engine and put it in drive, slowly easing the car away from the curb. I glance over at her, noticing the peaceful smile on her face as she sits there with her eyes closed.

"We'll be home soon, baby," I tell her, reaching over and sliding my palm against hers. She laces her fingers through mine and I gently squeeze her hand, resting it against her thigh. Isla sighs, her breathing growing heavier as she settles in her seat.

"Thank you, Logan," she whispers, her voice thick with sleep. "I'm really glad you showed up tonight, even if you did scare away one of my only friends."

My chest tightens and the thought of Silas with his arm around her shoulders instantly pisses me off. I swallow back the anger, focusing on her. She's here with me, her hand in mine, and not with him. "I told you he's not your friend, baby girl. He wants more from you... You see how well it works when guys try to be friends with you?"

Isla chuckles lightly, the smile spreading across her face. "Yeah, but that's different... it's you." She pauses and for a moment I think that maybe she fell asleep. "I don't want more with him. I've only ever wanted more with you."

My other hand grips the wheel tightly and I swallow hard over the lump that forms in my throat. As we pull up to a red light, I look back over at her, noticing that she is in fact asleep now. My heart swells as I replay her words in my head.

"I've only ever wanted more with you."
Me too, baby girl... me too.

CHAPTER ELEVEN
ISLA

"Isla, baby, wake up," Logan's soft voice snakes itself around my eardrums, instantly warming my soul as he wakes me from my drunken sleep. "We're home."

Slowly peeling my eyelids open, I look around, noticing that we're in the parking lot of the apartment building. I glance at Logan, meeting his clear eyes. He isn't as blurry as he was earlier when he showed up at the party and my head doesn't feel nearly as fuzzy as it did then.

"Are you able to walk?" he asks, his tone filled with nothing but compassion and concern.

I look at him and nod as a smile forms on my face. "I'm not going to lie, I felt pretty tipsy earlier, but I think that little nap I took definitely helped."

Logan chuckles, standing upright as he moves out of my way from the car door and offers me his hand. His palm is warm against mine as I slide my hand into his and he helps me out of the car. As I'm on my feet, I feel the instant rush to my head and I sway slightly on my feet. Okay, maybe I lied.

I don't feel as drunk as I did earlier, but my buzz is definitely still lingering.

Logan leads me out of the way so he can close the door and hits the lock button on his key fob. The headlights blink as the car beeps and he inches closer to me. In an instant, his hands are around my waist and he's lifting me into the air. I yelp as he takes me by surprise, but my legs instantly wrap around his waist as I link my arms behind his neck.

"I told you that I was fine to walk…"

Logan chuckles, his breath warm against my neck as he holds me tightly to his body. He begins to move, walking into the apartment building as he carries me. "I know, but this seemed like a much better idea."

"You're only saying that because you wanted to feel me close to you."

The words literally leave my mouth like word vomit and I'm instantly cringing at myself, embarrassed regardless of the alcohol in my system. I don't know what this is between us right now, but leave it to me to go ahead and make some dumb-ass comment like that.

"So, what if I do?" He breathes against my skin as he adjusts me in his arms to press the button to the elevator. "That not good with you, baby girl?"

I gulp, swallowing hard over the lump in my throat. "I'm good with that." I don't know how he manages to do it, but Logan has this effect on me that renders me essentially speechless. There's nothing bad about any of it, I just don't know how to act around him right now.

I had a crush on him for as long as I could remember. There was a point where I wasn't sure that he would ever feel the same way about me. I thought that I was just a distraction for him when he would kiss me and touch me in the dark, but now I'm faced with this new reality and I'm not sure how to fully process it.

There's a conversation we still need to have, but I don't think either of us are fully ready to dive into that. For now, I'm going to just go along with whatever this is and not question it. I have him back in my arms again and I'm not ready to ruin the moment and let him go... even if that means we become a secret again.

Logan carries me the whole way back to the apartment and doesn't put me down until we reach my bed. He gently lowers me down onto the mattress, pulling back the covers before he takes my shoes off for me.

"You know, I'm fully capable of doing that myself," I remind him, watching him as he kneels on the floor in front of me.

He glances up at me, his deep blue eyes piercing mine. "Why don't you just let me take care of you?"

I swallow hard and nod, giving him my feet as he pulls my socks off and tosses them onto the floor. He rises to his feet, walking over to my dresser to find me some pajamas, but I don't want to wear any of them right now. While his back is turned to me, I strip out of my pants and toss them onto the floor. Logan glances in the mirror by my bureau, his eyes finding mine as I reach for the bottom hem of my shirt.

"What are you up to?" he questions me, his voice low and husky. He slowly turns around to face me, staring at me with a darkened expression and a fire burning in his blue irises.

I pull my shirt off and throw it onto the floor. "Getting ready for bed," I tell him as I scoot closer to the headboard. Logan doesn't move from where he's standing across the room. "Can I wear your shirt to sleep in?" I ask him, my voice barely audible. "Like old times..."

His Adam's apple bobs as he swallows hard, but he nods and peels off his sweatshirt as he strides across the room toward me. I watch as it falls to the floor and he reaches behind his head and pulls his t-shirt over his head. He inches closer to the bed, stopping just beside it as he hands me his shirt.

I slip it over my head, feeling the warmth of it from his body. The smell of his cologne instantly fills my senses and I smile, feeling like I'm home. He lingers by the side of the bed, watching me as I find peace just in wearing his damn shirt. I glance up at him, my eyes finding the fire still burning in his oceanic depths.

"Lay with me?" I ask him quietly as I scoot to the other side to give him room. He pauses for a moment, like he's fighting an internal battle as he shifts his weight nervously. "August won't be home tonight, right?"

Logan nods, his shoulders sagging in relief as he remembers their conversation. He climbs into the bed, naked from the waist up with his sweatpants hugging his hips. I stare at the cut lines of his torso as his muscles move with his movements. He's perfectly sculpted, like a Greek god. He lies down beside me, instinctively sliding his arm under the back of my neck as he pulls me closer to him. I settle along his side, wrapping my arm around his waist as I rest my head on his chest.

Lifting my head, I prop my chin on his chest and stare up at him as he looks down at me. "What are we doing, Logan?"

His eyes bounce back and forth between mine. "I don't know, baby. Whatever feels right."

I stare at him, so desperately wanting to talk to him about this, but what am I supposed to say? He wanted to be friends and now he doesn't, but that doesn't exactly put a label on it. Who's to say he even wants more? Maybe that's something we shouldn't have. He's right... we're just doing whatever feels right and whatever comes of it, we will just have to deal with in the moment.

"Can I ask you something?" he says, his warm breath fanning across my face.

"Anything," I answer him honestly, although I'm a little nervous about the alcohol still in my system and the fact that I could have a case of word vomit at any moment right now.

He's silent for a second, his touch gentle as he

brushes a stray hair away from my face. "Do you have a thing for Silas?"

My eyebrows pinch together as I place my hands on his chest. "No. Why would you ask that?"

"I don't know," he whispers, shrugging lightly. "I've seen the two of you together and I just don't know… maybe he would be the better choice for you."

Lifting myself up, I inch closer to him, taking the sides of his face in my hands. Logan's eyes fall shut and he exhales deeply, a ragged breath coming from his chest. He slowly opens his eyelids, his blue eyes unreadable as he stares back at me. "There's no choice to be made," I tell him, softly stroking the sides of his face with my fingertips. "The choice was made for me when I first met you."

Logan chuckles softly, shaking his head. "You're a crazy girl, you know that?"

Crazy for you…

His hands find the sides of my head and he pulls me closer until our lips meet. We collide in an instant and I'm lost under his spell as his mouth moves against mine, bruising me with his touch. His tongue slides against the seam of my lips, parting them as he slips inside.

Our tongues dance together as we deepen the

kiss and he rolls us onto our sides. We lay together, his leg sliding between mine as I throw mine over his hip, moving even closer to him. A warmth spreads through the pit of my stomach and his thigh is warm as it presses against my center.

The friction makes me moan and I shift against him, feeling his body just beneath my panties. Logan's tongue slides against mine as his hands travel down my torso, slipping beneath the bottom hem of his shirt that I'm wearing.

"I fucking love you in my t-shirt," he murmurs against my lips as he sucks my bottom lip between his teeth. "You're the most beautiful thing that will ever grace my vision."

His lips collide with mine and he swallows my moans as I grind myself against his leg. His fingertips are light as they travel across my torso with featherlight touches. My breath catches in my throat as he touches the edge of my bra and pauses.

He pulls away slightly, his eyes searching mine. "Is this okay?" he asks softly, his bright blue irises dancing under the light of the moon that shines through my bedroom window.

Biting down on my bottom lip, I swallow my nerves and nod. "I don't want you to stop."

Logan slides his fingers along my bra, reaching

the top before diving under the cotton material. His palm is warm against my breast as he takes it in his hand, slowly tracing circles around my nipple. "Has anyone ever touched you like this before?"

I swallow hard as my cheeks burn under his gaze. "No."

"Fuck," he murmurs, his eyes soft on mine. "So sweet and so innocent..."

He pauses, the corners of his lips curling upward.

"And all mine."

CHAPTER TWELVE
LOGAN

The thought alone of no one touching her like this before has me ready to come in my pants. Isla writhes under my touch as I play with her nipples, slowly circling them with my fingers before rolling them between my fingertips. Pressing my lips to hers, I swallow her moans as she grinds herself against my leg, looking for some kind of relief.

Abandoning her breasts, I slide my hand down her torso, reaching the waistband of her panties. I hear the sharp intake of her breath as I slip beneath them, gently touching the sensitive part of her. "If it's too much, just tell me to stop."

Isla pulls her face away from mine, nodding as her lips part slightly. I slide a finger through the wetness that pools between her legs and circle it around her clit. Her hips buck involuntarily as I play with her, working my fingers around the sensitive bundle of nerves. I watch her face, the pink tint taking over her cheeks as her breathing grows ragged and shallow.

My movements are slow and gentle as I slowly slide a finger inside her. Her eyes widen and a soft moan falls from her full lips as I begin to move it in and out of her. Pressing my palm against her clit, I apply pressure, rubbing her as I fuck her with my hand.

"Oh my god, Logan," she breathes, her voice hoarse, and she grinds against my palm as her face screws up. She stops moving against me, her eyes searching mine as she reaches for the top of my sweatpants. "I want to touch you too, but I've never done this before. Tell me how to make you feel good."

All of the blood in my body instantly rushes to my already hard cock. Jesus fucking Christ, what is this girl doing to me? The thought of telling her what to do and how to make me come has me coming apart at the seams.

Lifting my hips, I use my free hand to push down my sweatpants and boxers, freeing my erection. Isla looks down at me, swallowing hard as her eyes travel across my body. She slides her hand closer to my cock and slowly wraps her delicate fingers around my length. She looks back up at me for approval, her eyes searching mine for some type of direction.

"I'll show you, baby girl," I murmur, keeping my one hand pressed against her pussy with my finger still inside her as I take my other hand and wrap it around hers. Tightening my grip around her, I slowly move her fist up and down my cock, her soft palm stroking me.

A moan vibrates in my chest and I shift my hips as my balls begin to constrict. "You're so good," I murmur, praising her as she continues to stroke me under my guidance. I begin to move her hand faster as a warmth spreads across my abdomen and she falls into a steady rhythm. "That's it, baby. Don't fucking stop."

I let her take over, moving my hand away as I begin to work my other one against her, grinding my palm onto her clit as I slide my finger in and out of her. She strokes my cock just like I showed her and goddamn, I swear this girl was made for me.

Grabbing the back of her head, I crash my lips to hers, swallowing her sounds as she comes undone. I push her closer and closer to the edge as she slides her hand along my length, my balls drawing closer to my body as I feel my release approaching.

We're both lost in the moment when we hear the front door slam shut. The sound echoes through the apartment and we both freeze. Isla quickly releases me, grabbing for the blankets in a frenzy as I jump out of the bed. I'm rushing toward her bedroom door, pulling up my pants as I hear footsteps shuffling in the kitchen.

"Logan!" August slurs, calling out for me as he knocks something over in the living room. "Bro. You're never going to believe what happened."

Fuck.

"What the hell is he doing here?" Isla whispers, her voice panicked. "I thought he wasn't coming home tonight."

As I move into the doorway of her room, I look back at her, holding my fingers against my lips. "Just pretend to be asleep, okay? I'll handle this."

Isla nods, pulling the covers up to her chin as she rolls over to face the other way. I quickly slip out of her room, softly shutting the door behind me as I walk across the hall, heading to my room. Just as I'm opening the door to go inside, August reaches the opposite end of the hallway.

"Oh good, you're awake," he sighs, running a hand through his tousled hair. I look at him, my eyebrows drawing together as I notice a cut on the side of his head and a bruise already forming under his eye. "Is Isla asleep?"

I nod, narrowing my eyes at him. "What the fuck happened to you?"

"I gotta take a piss," he mumbles, stumbling past me as he heads toward the bathroom. "Meet me in the kitchen with a bottle of Jack for story time."

August disappears into the bathroom and I sigh as I walk past Isla's room and head into the kitchen to find a bottle of Jack. Leave it to August to decide to come home and fuck this all up. He didn't seem suspicious, so that's a good thing, but what we're doing is risky.

Too fucking risky...

CHAPTER THIRTEEN
ISLA

Rolling over in bed, I slowly peel open my eyelids and squint against the bright sunlight that shines through my bedroom window. My head pounds, screaming in protest at the sun that burns the sclerae of my eyes. I roll the other way, burying my face in the pillows as I block out the harsh light.

I shouldn't have drank as much as I did last night, but it was my first time at a college party, so what the hell. You only live once, right? My memory from the night is still a little fuzzy and I bury myself under the covers as I sift through my thoughts.

It all comes crashing down on me like a ton of bricks as I piece everything together. I remember being at the party, sitting with Silas when Logan showed up. He was pissed, seeing the two of us together and scared Silas away.

"I don't know how to be your friend, Isla."

"What if I don't want you to play the part anymore?"

Logan pulled me into the laundry room and kissed me like it was the first time we had ever touched. I cringe, a heat creeping up my neck and spreading across my cheeks as I replay the chain of events that went down after he took me home. Logan taking me to bed, his fingers inside me and my hand around his cock. *Jesus Christ.* Drunk me has more balls than I've ever had.

"You're so good."

"That's it, baby, don't fucking stop."

Oh my god. I really just hooked up with Logan Knight...

My brother's best friend.

Groaning, I throw the covers off of me and climb out of bed. I look down, noticing that I'm still wearing his t-shirt that he gave me last night. I quickly shuffle across my room, kicking his sweatshirt under my bed as I find that on my floor. Pulling open my drawers, I pull out a pair of sweatpants and slip them on, before grabbing a shirt of my own from my closet.

I shove Logan's t-shirt under my bed with his sweatshirt before slipping on one of my own shirts. Glancing in the mirror by my dresser, I notice the smeared makeup across my face and hastily wipe it away from under my eyes. Grabbing my hair, I twist it onto a bun on top of my head and wrap a hair tie around it. I look like shit, but I'm not sure that I care with how hungover I feel right now.

My stomach churns and I know I need to find something to eat. Maybe some water. I don't know, I just know that this feeling needs to go away. That and the embarrassment of what happened last night. Thank God Logan left my room before August found him in here. He wasn't even supposed to come home last night, so we got lucky with the way it played out.

Although, there is a part of me that doesn't feel good about how it went down. Logan slipped out of my room like nothing happened and I didn't see him after that. All it took was one moment, one close call with my brother, and I'm back to being Logan's dirty little secret.

Sighing in defeat, I slowly open the door to my bedroom and slip out into the hallway as I make my way out into the kitchen. As I walk in, I notice August sitting at the dining room table with his face in his arms. A plate of pancakes sits in the center of the table untouched.

Bypassing him, I walk into the kitchen and find Logan in there handwashing some dishes in the sink. My eyes travel across the planes of his naked back, watching the way his muscles move as he works his hands in the soapy water. He's still wearing the same sweatpants he had on last night and they hang low around his waist.

He glances over his shoulder as I pull open the refrigerator door and grab the orange juice from inside. "Hey you," he smiles, his voice soft as his eyes search mine. "How did you sleep last night?"

My face instantly heats up under his gaze and I turn my back to him as I grab a glass from the cabinet and pour myself some of the juice. "Fine, thanks," I mumble, turning back around to face him as I take a drink. "How about you?"

Logan smirks, shrugging. "I imagine that I could have slept better, but I don't have any complaints."

I practically choke on my orange juice as he winks at me before turning back to the dishes in front of him. I'm glad he turned back around because I'm pretty sure I would melt to a puddle on the floor if he kept looking at me the way he does with those ocean blue eyes of his.

"I made breakfast, if you're hungry," he offers as he rinses off a plate. "I don't know if August is asleep or what the hell he's doing out there."

Grabbing my glass of juice, I slip out of the kitchen and step back into the dining room. As I pull out one of the chairs, August lifts his head, his bloodshot eyes finding mine. My face contorts as I notice an angry cut on the side of his forehead and the black and blue bruise under his eye.

"What the hell happened to you?"

"Jesus," he groans, dropping his head to his hands. "Can you keep your voice down? I have the fucking hangover from hell right now."

Logan slips into the room, taking a seat across from me as he sits down a steaming mug of coffee in front of himself. "I'm sure it doesn't help that you got your ass beat last night too."

Narrowing my eyes, I look back and forth between the two of them. "Is someone going to tell me what happened? You have a fucking game today, August," I scold him, directing my angry gaze on him. "What the hell were you thinking?"

"Obviously, I wasn't thinking, *Mom*," he growls

at me, lifting his head as his gaze finds mine. "It was just a misunderstanding."

Logan chuckles as he takes a sip of his coffee and sets the mug back down. "Your genius brother over here didn't realize that the girl he planned on going home with had a boyfriend." He pauses, shaking his head as he rolls his eyes. "Her boyfriend walked in on them making out on the couch and decided to drag August outside before introducing him to his fist."

"You've got to be kidding me." I look at August, the disappointment hanging heavily in my voice. "What happened to your only focus being on hockey? First you were fucking around with Poppy and now you're going after girls who have boyfriends?"

"I didn't fucking know," he snaps, cutting his eyes at me. August sighs in defeat, his shoulders sagging. "Shit. You're right. I'm letting myself get distracted and it's going to bite me in the ass soon. I'm already in hot water with Coach for being late to practice."

My stomach grumbles and I finally take a pancake, sliding it onto my plate. We're all silent for a moment, both of them watching me as I put some butter and syrup on my food before shoveling some into my mouth. "You need to get your shit together, August."

"Yeah, I know," he mumbles, taking a drink of the glass of water in front of him before he looks at Logan. "You're smart for not getting involved with anyone, bro. Seriously, it's not worth the bullshit that comes with it. I need to be like you and keep my head down and just focus on hockey."

A piece of my pancake gets lodged in my throat and I cough, choking on it as Logan glances at me from the rim of his mug. He slowly takes a sip, not saying anything as I finally swallow down the piece of food that was stuck.

"Seriously, Knight," August goes on, after giving me a weird look for choking on my food. I blame it on him, though, because what the fuck? "You'd be a fucking idiot to get involved with someone right now. We gotta think about our futures—our careers that we're working toward. The league is the only thing that matters."

Logan nods, but stays silent as he fills his plate with food. I've suddenly lost my appetite and want to go crawl back in my bed. I didn't expect him to come out and tell August about last night, but the way he doesn't say anything to him confuses me. It's almost as if he agrees with everything August is saying right now.

Hockey has always come first for Logan and I was an idiot to forget that—even if it was only for a night.

"You're coming to the game tonight, right?" August asks me as he finally gets himself a pancake. "Mom and Dad are driving in for the night."

"Yeah, I'll be there," I tell him, feeling Logan's eyes on me, but I avoid his gaze as I finish the food on my plate. "Good luck explaining that shiner you got to Mom."

"Fuck," August groans, tilting his head backward dramatically. "She's going to be all over my shit about it. You don't say a word to her about it, Isla. Let me handle it."

I raise my hands in submission as I push my chair back and stand up from my seat. "I know nothing." Grabbing my plate, I turn away from them and leave it on the counter in the kitchen. "I'm going to go back to sleep for a little bit. I'll see you guys tonight at the game."

August nods, shoveling food into his mouth, and I chance a look at Logan as I walk back through the dining room. His lips part, like he wants to say something, but instead he clamps them shut and toys with his mug of coffee in front of him.

Pushing my shoulders back, I lift my chin and direct my gaze away from him, even though the pain from his dismissal snakes its way into my heart. I leave the two of them in the dining room as I slip back into my room and climb into my bed.

Fuck you and your silence, Logan Knight.

CHAPTER FOURTEEN
LOGAN

The cold air from inside the rink slides across my skin as soon as my skates hit the ice. Everyone else is already skating around, stretching as we warm up for the game, shooting the shit with each other. I skate past August as he replays what happened last night before sending a puck soaring through the air toward our goalie.

It hits the edge of the net, the loud ping of metal sounding through the air before it sends the puck in the opposite direction of the goal. Usually, I would talk some shit to August or whoever is near me, but right now, I have no desire to.

I don't want to hear about last night, not after the way my balls still ache. And definitely not after the way Isla looked at me this morning. I fucked up, siding with her brother's bullshit when I should have just came clean. Instead, I chose to cover up my tracks and completely dismissed what happened with Isla before August showed up.

She wasn't happy with me and I should have taken the time to go talk to her before we had to leave, but I chose to give her space instead. I don't know what the fuck I'm doing here. I skate past Cameron, one of our players on defense, ignoring him as he calls out to me to pass him the puck. I need to make things right with Isla after last night.

I just don't know how I'm going to make it up to her.

"Dude," Cam skates over to me, slamming his shoulder against mine as he catches me off guard. He knocks me off balance, but I quickly recover as I glare at him. "What's going on with you?"

"Nothing."

Cam rolls his eyes, stealing the puck from me as he begins to skate backward. "You better get your shit together before the game starts. You know Coach won't hesitate to bench you."

My jaw clenches and I keep my eyes trained on him as I skate toward him. He's right. Even though I'm pissed off and frustrated, I need to focus on what we're here to do. Instead, I'm going to have to channel my anger and use it to my advantage... and pray I don't wind up getting myself kicked out of the game for taking it too far.

The shit with Isla is going to have to wait until after the game. I'll just talk to her afterward and try to sort it all out. I swallow hard over the lump that forms from the thought alone. Maybe August was right...

When it comes down to it, hockey will always come first.

———

After warm-ups, the ice is cleared off and the announcer calls all of our names as we skate back out into the arena. The crowd is loud, cheering as we line up against the opposing team. We have the advantage, being the home team, but the team we're playing tonight is ruthless. It's going to be one hell of a game for the season opener.

As they get set up for the face-off, I take my place along the blue line in the defense spot, my eyes scanning the stands as we wait for the ref to drop the puck. I find my mom first, her smile huge as she waves at me from where she's sitting with the Whitleys. I return her grin, although I'm not sure she sees it through the cage blocking my face.

My eyes continue down the line, scanning right past August's mom and dad before landing on *her*. I would be lying if I said there wasn't a part of me that was wondering if she would even show tonight. She wouldn't miss it for her brother, but I wouldn't be surprised if she wanted to miss it because of me. Her eyes meet mine from across the ice and I don't miss the way that the pink tint spreads across her cheeks.

She might be pissed off at me still, but even now, I can still see the evident effect that I have on her. The ref drops the puck, and I tear my gaze away from Isla as August wins the face-off and sends the black disc in my direction. It flies past the right wing in front of me and I stop it with my stick as it ends up in my zone.

Pushing off on my skates, I slide across the ice, stickhandling the puck as I glance back and forth at the boards. August is in the center where it's too congested. Sterling, our right wing, has someone on him already. When I glance over to the left, I notice that Cam is open and pass the puck to him as the other team's right wing reaches me.

Cam spins the puck around with him, keeping it with him along the blade of his stick. I hang back, watching him as he takes it toward the opposing goal. August skates down with him with Sterling in his zone as they close in on the offensive side. Cam passes the puck to August, but their defensive line is right there and he doesn't have a clear shot.

August passes it to Sterling, who makes a last-ditch effort, sending the puck flying at the goaltender. He blocks it, deflecting the shot as it slides back across the ice. One of the offensive players on the other team grabs the puck and starts skating in my direction.

I begin skating backward, before turning around and making my way farther into my zone. Glancing over, I notice Leander, one of our other defensemen skating to the other side of the net. Number 15, from the other team, skates directly toward me, getting closer to our net. I attempt to block his shot, but he fakes me out and passes it to another teammate. Slamming my shoulder into him, I check him anyway, because fuck that shit.

He yells some obscenities at me and I spin around as I see the puck miss our net. Number 15 skates after it and I'm hot on his tail. He slides around the back of the net with the puck, attempting to sneak it past Asher, our goaltender, as he makes his way to the front. Asher blocks it and

Number fucking 15 slashes his stick at Asher, bringing it down on his arm before knocking his shoulder into him.

"What the fuck!" I yell, looking for the ref as Number 15 skates past me with a smirk. Out of impulse and anger, I slide my stick toward him, hooking it around his skate, effectively tripping him as he stumbles for a moment. "You better fucking call him for slashing!"

The ref blows his whistle, pointing his finger at me instead. My blood boils as I get a goddamn penalty for tripping, even though they completely disregarded Number 15 slashing Asher. I'm fucking pissed, fucking livid as I skate over to the box to sit out for my two-minute penalty.

I watch as the five players on the other team play against our four for their power play and I'm ready to go out there and bash some skulls in. My eyes are glued to Number 15, watching as he skates around, smirking in my direction every time he passes like he won.

Oh hell no... he has no idea what's coming for him.

It feels like forever, sitting in here for two minutes, but I watch our team as we somehow score a goal. The victorious feeling doesn't last long as the other team scores on our net and then the power play is over and I'm back on the ice. I skate over to the bench for a shift change, watching the rink for Number 15 to enter again.

When he finally hops the boards and gets back out there, I'm standing up, yelling shift change for one of our defensive players to switch with me. No one bothers to argue or attempts to stop me. They all saw the way he slashed Asher's arm and if there's anyone going out there to handle business, it's me—the enforcer.

I hang back in my zone, waiting for the perfect moment to arise, when Number 15 starts skating back in my direction with the puck. My skates slide across the ice as I meet him right outside of my zone, slamming my body into him with a clean hit. There's nothing for the ref to call, but he's fucking pissed.

He narrows his eyes at me through the cage of his helmet before skating back toward me. As he reaches me, I shake my gloves off, tossing them to the ground as I lift my fists up to my face. Number 15 mirrors my actions, his gloves dropping as he gets in my space, and it's on. He's the first to throw a punch, but his fist connects with the side of my helmet, no doubt hurting him more than it hurt me.

Wrapping my arm around his shoulders, I bend him over and grip the back of his helmet with my hand and rip it off his head. He shoves at my chest as I drop his helmet onto the ice and we break apart for a moment.

"You fucking dick," he growls, coming back at me as he reaches for my helmet. He doesn't anticipate the hit coming for him as I drive my fist into the side of his face. He rips my helmet away from my head and delivers a blow right across my jaw, instantly splitting my lip open.

I wrap my arms around his waist, skating him backward into the board before rearing back and slamming my fist into his face again. Blood spurts from his nose and just as I'm about to hit him again, we're getting ripped apart by the two refs. Running my tongue over my teeth, I taste blood and smile at him.

"Both of you—in the fucking box, now!" the ref shouts at us, pointing his finger toward the penalty box. Laughing, I shake my head and grab my gloves and helmet from the ice before skating over to the box.

I catch my mom and Isla staring at me from their seats and I raise my hand up to them. Fuck it, if they're both going to be present for my games, I might as well give them all a show. Shrugging to myself, I climb into the box and take my respective seat.

Number 15 fucked up when he slashed at Asher and got away with it.

I don't regret a single thing from the fight, because that's what you do for family, for those that mean the world to you.

You go to fucking war for them.

CHAPTER FIFTEEN
ISLA

The restaurant is relatively quiet when I first get there with my parents. Camilla, Logan's mom, is already here and seated at the table. The three of us sit down with her, placing an order for our drinks as we wait for August and Logan to get here after getting showered and changed after their game.

"How is everything going, Isla?" my father asks me as my mother and Camilla fall into a quiet conversation among themselves. I haven't really spoken to my father much since I moved here for school, although I'm sure that my mother has kept him well-informed.

I shrug, giving him a small smile. "It's been an adjustment, but it's all going well. I've been enjoying my classes so far and have made a few friends."

"Good." He smiles, flashing his white teeth at me. "I know it isn't what you're used to, but I feel better knowing you're living with your brother and Logan."

Grabbing the glass of water in front of me, I take a long sip, swallowing hard before nodding. "Yeah, it's been nice having them around."

"Have the two of them been staying out of trouble?"

My eyes widen slightly. I've never been a very good liar and tend to give it away on my face every single time. I'm about to answer him, when August and Logan come striding toward the table, both of them sporting matching black and blue eyes. "Why don't you ask them yourself?" I smile softly, glancing down at the menu in front of me in an effort to avoid the entire conversation.

"August..." My father's voice is low, his tone scolding. "What the hell happened to your face?"

I lift my head as my mother gasps and August and Logan both sit on opposite sides of me at the table. All three sets of eyes from our parents are on August, assessing the damage that was done to his pretty face. Logan snorts and grabs a menu before he begins to look at it.

"I may or may not have gotten into a fight," August offers, a crooked grin forming on his face. He picks up his glass of water and takes a sip. "It's no big deal, though. Everything is good."

"No big deal?" my father snaps at him, slamming his menu down on the table. Camilla tears her eyes from August, glancing at Logan before she looks at my mother. She shakes her head in disappointment and sighs. "You do know that anything you do off the ice can also affect your play time, right? I hope you realize how much is at stake here with these little mishaps you've been having. I wasn't going to say anything, because I know that you've been doing better, but I heard about you being late to practice."

August narrows his eyes at him. "How do you know that?"

"That's beside the point. August, you need to take this seriously. I don't know what happened, but college seems to have been the worst thing for you."

"Dennis," my mother says softly, her hand reaching for his on the table. "Why don't you give him a chance to speak?"

My father glances at my mother, his eyes wild

with rage, but she instantly brings him back, calming him as he stares at her for a moment. His eyes fall shut and he inhales deeply before opening them again and looking at August. "What's going on, August?"

No one needs to address Logan's face because we all witnessed the fight he got into on the ice. It was a little more aggressive than necessary, but he was clearly working through something... but I'm the only one who knows what is troubling his mind.

August shrugs as he nervously plays with the napkin in front of him. "Sometimes shit just feels heavy, you know? I don't know, I guess I was enjoying myself a little too much. But I realized that I've been on the path to jeopardizing everything and have turned things around."

"He's been doing well," I offer, interjecting when I know it's not my place, but I hate seeing my brother shrinking under our father's scrutinizing gaze. "He got a little distracted, but I've seen him making changes already."

It's a little white lie and I can feel Logan's eyes on the side of my face, but our parents don't need to know that. They don't need to know that he literally just got that shiner last night. I know my brother well enough to be able to trust him and believe him when he says he's going to make changes and do better. I believed him this morning and I need them to believe it too.

"I know how college can be," our father says, glancing between the three of us. "There are many distractions, you're trying to figure out where you're going in life, and the two of you are juggling a demanding sport. But, both of you have a future that can be built off of how well you perform while you're in college. I can't have you forgetting that, August. Both of you," he pauses, looking at August and Logan, "have so much riding on what happens over the next two years. Don't fuck it up."

Logan all but chokes on his water, August looks like he wants the floor to open up and swallow him whole, and I'm sitting here feeling awkward as hell. Logan's father wasn't around since he was a baby. My dad took Logan under his wing and was the closest thing he had to a father growing up. He has always had high expectations for him, just like he does for August.

I feel bad for both of them, listening to them get scolded like children, but honestly, my brother needs this. Maybe not Logan as much, because he weirdly seems like he's become the more responsible out of the two. These are the moments in my life that I really hate hockey and what it does to some people.

August and Logan are more than just the star players everyone gets caught up in viewing them as.

My mother interjects, telling the boys how they both played so well at the game and how much she enjoyed being able to come watch their first game of the season. Camilla does the same, but makes sure she slides in a little remark about how Logan was a little out of hand with the fight.

He doesn't say anything in return, and our server arrives back at the perfect time to take all of our orders for food. Everyone takes their turn, telling the server, and she thanks us before she disappears into the back of the restaurant. Everyone falls into a lighter conversation as we move away from the topic of August's recent indiscretions.

I can feel the tension radiating off Logan as he falls silent, keeping to himself most of the night instead of engaging in the conversation. I don't miss the way that Camilla gives her son questioning looks throughout our meal. She knows that something is off with him too, but she doesn't bring it up in front of everyone. I'm the reason why he's behaving the way he is.

If he wouldn't have just blindly agreed with my

brother this morning, things wouldn't be like this between us. Although, he used it to his advantage tonight and I can't help but feel a sense of pride after seeing him play. He played his ass off, even though he got into a pretty gnarly fight, and he still had the spotlight on him during the game.

Shaking my head to myself, I push the thoughts out of my mind. I've let Logan cloud my mind for far too long and even though I don't want to, maybe I need to just let him go completely. As much as I want to explore more with him, the way he acted this morning left a bad taste in my mouth and I can't let myself forget about that.

If he was so concerned with my brother and their friendship, he would say something to him before he finds out about us. Logan was making no attempt at opening the doors for that conversation, so it only makes sense that he was just using me again like he used to. He wasn't pulling the same destructive shit that my brother was, but in his own way, he wasn't doing anything better. He was just using me as a distraction and I deserve more than that.

I refuse to be anyone's distraction or dirty secret anymore.

It's time that I stand up for myself and have

some self-respect.

We all finish up dinner and head outside for goodbyes and hugs before parting ways. My parents climb in their car as Camilla disappears over to her own. August slides behind the wheel of his car and I hop into the back as Logan gets into the passenger's side. My parents picked me up earlier and gave me a ride to the game before dinner, so it only made sense for me to ride home with August and Logan now.

"Talk about a shit show of a dinner," August mutters as he pulls the car out of the parking lot. He glances at me through the rearview mirror and narrows his eyes. "You know, it would have been nice for you to give me a heads-up that dad was going to rip me a new asshole."

My eyebrows pinch together as my face scrunches up in distaste. "Or you could just get your shit together so you wouldn't have to have anyone on your ass about the dumb decisions you've been making lately." I pause for a moment, sighing as I shake my head. "I didn't know he was going to say anything, but you had to have known he would be coming for your jugular after seeing your black and blue eye."

August frowns. "Yeah, I know. I'm sorry, I know it isn't your fault. And honestly, I had it coming. I know I need to keep my head down and keep my focus on hockey, like Logan." August glances over at him, who has been silent the entire ride, staring out the window. "Seriously, bro. I haven't seen you with a girl except for your random hookups. How do you not let yourself get attached?"

"Would you really say you have any attachments?" Logan questions him, still staring out the window. "Other than Poppy, you've always just been playing the field."

"Ugh, don't even start with that Poppy shit. I'm pretty sure she's never going to talk to me again."

Logan shrugs, glancing at August before he looks back out the window. "Maybe that's a good thing. Less distractions, less attachments."

"You're right," August agrees with him and my stomach rolls as I try to block both of them out. "I'm gonna follow your lead from now on."

I all but choke on the breath that gets caught in my throat. August really has no idea what his best friend has been doing behind his back and I'm quite certain he never will know. It's better that he doesn't at this point, because Logan has made his stance evidently clear.

It was all a mistake.

And it's never going to happen again.

CHAPTER SIXTEEN
LOGAN

It's been two weeks since I found myself in Isla's bed. Two weeks since we've had a real conversation. And if I'm being honest, living in the same apartment as her is beginning to drive me mad. There's only so many nights in a week for me to go out with the guys and forget about her, but I can't let myself lose focus on what I'm really doing here.

She's become such a distraction, even though she's turned into a mute around me.

I don't even know how to approach the conversation with her. Do I start with an apology? I know what Isla really wants from me and I can't give her that. I'm not ready to ruin my friendship with my best friend, even if that means I can't have her.

All of this is completely fucked and it's fucking with my head every single day.

Isla has been distant and more withdrawn. She talks to her brother, but as soon as I walk into the room, she suddenly has something she has to go do, almost like she can't stand being around me. I don't blame her, because I feel the same damn way.

It's a complete contradiction. I want to be around her, to spend time with her, but knowing I can't have every part of her only makes it worse. It makes me want as much distance between us as possible. And every time I catch sight of her at school and I see her with that douchebag friend of hers, I want to put my fist directly through his face.

My jealousy is unwarranted because she isn't mine to be protective of. But if she can't be mine, she can't be anyone else's.

As I get off the ice and head back to the locker room, the thought of Isla and Silas plays through my head. I stood in the corridor of the building today, watching him as he opened the passenger-side door for her and helped her into his massive Jeep. Just thinking about his hands on her has me seeing red. Blood red.

I drop down onto one of the benches and set my stick down beside me before unlacing my skates.

Cam comes strolling in and sits down next to me, facing the other direction as he sets down his gloves and helmet. "You good, Knight?" he asks me, glancing at me from the corner of his eye.

After sliding my feet out of my skates, I take off my helmet and set it down on the bench. "I've just had a lot on my mind lately."

"Who is she?" Cam questions me as he puts the skate guards on the blades of his skates. I whip my head to the side, narrowing my eyes at him as he raises his eyebrows. "Come on, man. You can tell me."

I swallow hard over the lump lodged in my throat. There's no way in hell I can tell him. Shit, I can't tell anyone about this. August walks over to us, pulling the tape off of the blade of his stick as he drops down onto the bench across from us.

"There is no girl, Cam," August tells him as he begins to wrap fresh tape around the end of his stick. "Trust me, I live with him. I would know if there was a girl causing problems."

"Yeah, there's no girl."

Cam narrows his eyes, his lips pursed as he shakes his head. "I don't know. There's definitely something going on with you and my best guess is it has to do with a chick."

August raises an eyebrow at me. "You know, now that Cam says it, you have been kind of weird lately. You got a girl that you're hiding from all of us?"

What the fuck.

My breath catches in my throat and I quickly force a laugh as I rise to my feet and grab my shit. "Seriously, there's no girl. I've just been worried about my grades lately." It's a lie, but neither of them need to know that. I just need the two of them to shut up.

I go to grab my stick and just as I'm about to carry it to my locker, August grabs the other end of it. Dread fills the pit of my stomach as my gaze meets his. We're both holding opposite ends of the hockey stick and I'm paralyzed by fear that he's not going to let the topic of a girl go.

"Dude, let go," he says, his eyebrows drawing close together. "I thought you wanted me to re-tape your stick for you?"

Letting out the breath I didn't realize I was holding, relief floods me. "Shit, I forgot," I admit, shaking my head as I let go of the stick and he takes it from me. I glance at Cam as he walks away from us, heading back to his locker.

August narrows his eyes at me. "I know your grades are fine. What's really going on?"

Shifting my weight nervously, I say the first thing that comes to my head that isn't Isla. "My mom said that Elias reached out to her, asking for my number."

"Elias? Like... your dad?"

I haven't told anyone. Hell, I haven't even really talked to my mom about it. She mentioned it to me in private after dinner and told me to think about it and let her know. I haven't thought about it until this moment because I had to detach myself from it completely. He left when I was six fucking months old. Why the hell was he reaching out now?

"Yeah, him."

"Shit," August sighs, his eyes filling with sympathy. "I'm sorry, bro. I had no idea. Are you going to talk to him?"

I shrug. "I don't know yet." It's not a lie, because I really don't know. He's a stranger in my eyes, so what could he possibly want from me? I hope it's not a father-son relationship, because that ship sailed decades ago when he left without a single phone call or letter.

August frowns as he begins to wrap the tape around the blade of my stick. "Let's go grab a beer or something after we're done here. We can talk about it then, if you want to, or else we can just get shit-faced instead."

Smiling at him, I take my stick and nod. "Sounds like a plan to me."

———

I swear, August is on some type of self-sabotaging path, because we end up at the sports bar where Poppy works at. She sees us as we come in and quickly moves to the other side of the bar as the other bartender helps us out. August opens a tab and orders us both a beer. His eyes are on Poppy but she doesn't bother turning around to look at him.

"Did you know she was going to be working?" I ask him as Amanda, the other bartender, sets our glasses in front of us. "I thought you were trying to avoid any type of attachments."

August shrugs as he takes a gulp of the hoppy liquid. "I don't know her schedule, but I was hoping she would be here. Just because I don't want anything with her doesn't mean I don't like to check in on her from time to time."

"You know you sound a lot like a stalker, right?"

August cuts his eyes to me. "If I'm doing it in the

open, does that really make me a stalker? I'm not, like, following her around and shit. I just like to drop in for a beer every now and then."

Rolling my eyes, I shake my head as I grab the menu in front of us. "Have you tried to talk to her? I feel like that crosses some kind of boundary."

"Nah, I'm pretty positive that she wants nothing to do with me. I mean, I did tell her upfront that it was just going to be a no-strings-attached kind of thing and she was down for it." August pauses for a moment, wrapping his hands around his glass as he wipes away the condensation. "I don't know, man. If she tells me to stop coming here, though, I'll respect her wishes and stop showing up."

Our bartender walks back over to us, taking our order as we each opt for some wings. August downs the rest of his glass and she takes it to refill it as I continue to sip on mine. August seems like he's the one who wants to come here to drown his sorrows instead of me.

"You wanna talk about the shit with your dad?" he asks, and I silently thank him for not prying into it any more. This is how our friendship has always been and I honestly love him for it. August is more of an open book. He'll share things without you having to dig deep for answers. Me, on the other hand, I keep my cards close and don't say much unless I really want to.

And right now, I don't want to talk about any of that. "Nah," I tell him, shaking my head. "I need more time to process it myself I think before I'm ready to talk about it."

August nods, picking up his fresh beer as he takes a sip of it. "I get it, bro. Whenever you're ready to talk about it, I'm here."

"Thanks, August," I tell him, clasping his shoulder with my hand as I give it a squeeze. "You're the best friend I could ever ask for."

"And don't you ever forget that shit," he says, laughing as he lifts up his glass to cheers with me. I tap mine against his, the glass clinking, before we both swallow some of the liquid. I drain the rest of my glass and set it down for our bartender to refill it.

We fall into a comfortable conversation as we get our wings and another beer. We mostly talk shop, talking shit about hockey and the gossip from the guys. Believe it or not, guys gossip, too, and August has all of the tea on our teammates.

As we're eating, I see Silas take a seat on the other side of the bar. He doesn't notice us and even if he did, we're not friends with him so there would be no reason to interact. Seeing him makes me think of her and the thoughts begin to spiral. She left with him after school, was she with him until he came here?

"Okay, who pissed in your beer?" August questions me, his eyes following my gaze across the bar. "Isn't that Isla's friend?"

I nod, dropping the bones of my wing onto my plate. "What do you think of him? She's been spending a lot of time with him."

"I don't know. I don't really know the guy." August turns to look at me, raising an eyebrow. "Why are you so worried about who she's hanging out with?"

I swallow hard over the knives in my throat and grab my beer to wash it down. Don't fuck this up now, Logan. Act cool.

Shrugging, I set my beer down, plastering an impassive look on my face. "I'm not. He just seems like a douche and I don't want to see her get hurt by him or something."

"Mhm," he murmurs, his eyes still assessing me as if he doesn't believe a single word that comes out of my mouth right now. "Well, you don't need to worry about her. I'll make sure she's good. And if he does anything, I'll fucking break his hands."

"Yeah, of course," I say, nodding as I fill my

mouth with more beer. August's eyes linger on the side of my face for a moment and I can't help but feel like I've already given too much away. I don't like the way he's looking at me, like he knows my secret or something.

The thing is... he has no fucking clue.

CHAPTER SEVENTEEN
ISLA

I'm on the couch watching a movie as my brother and Logan come stumbling in through the door. Sitting up, I look over the back of the cushion after pausing my movie and watch them move into the living room. August can barely stand up, but Logan looks like he's in better shape than my brother.

"Did you guys drink everything they had at the bar?" I ask, shaking my head in disapproval at my brother's current state. He doesn't look like he's enjoying how drunk he is. Instead, his eyes meet mine and they're bloodshot like he was crying. "What's wrong, August?"

"Fucking Poppy," he slurs, stumbling farther into the room. He rounds the couch and collapses onto the chaise lounge of the sectional. "She has a boyfriend already."

"What happened?"

August sighs and the smell of stale beer reaches my nose, even though he's not that close to me. "We went to the bar and she was working. I didn't plan on talking to her, but you know, I did. And she told me about her boyfriend, who then fucking showed up to pick her up. So, that's pretty cool."

My eyebrows draw together and I frown as I stare at him with nothing but sympathy. I hate seeing my brother hurt, but he had to have known this would happen eventually. "I thought you were the one who didn't want anything with her. You told her no attachments, right?"

"Yeah, but fuck, Isla. That doesn't mean I meant what I said." August pauses, burping loudly as he rolls over to face the opposite direction. "I'm just gonna go to sleep."

I turn off the movie I was watching and put on the NHL channel for him before turning down the volume so it isn't so loud. August is already snoring by the time I grab a blanket and drape it over him. Taking a step back, I wrap my arms around myself as I watch him sleeping with a broken heart. August is complex as hell. He acts like he doesn't need anyone, but I think he actually had feelings for Poppy.

As I lift my eyes from him, I find Logan leaning against the wall with his hands tucked in the front pockets of his joggers as he watches me. His gaze meets mine, but he doesn't move a muscle as he continues to watch me. I swallow hard, feeling the heat creeping up my neck and spreading across my cheeks.

"Um, I'm going to head to bed too," I tell him, my voice sounding completely unnatural as I clear my throat. I don't owe him an explanation. Hell, we haven't talked in like two weeks now, but being under his watchful eye, I still feel like I need to explain myself.

Logan doesn't utter a single word, he just nods as he watches me walk around the couch and head down the hallway. Just as I'm reaching for the handle of my door, I feel his hand wrap around my wrist.

"Isla," he says softly, his voice tender and gentle. "Can we please talk?"

I turn my body slightly, but not completely, my eyes meeting his bright blue irises as they bounce back and forth between mine. He has this effect on me, where all it takes is this look, the sound of his voice, and I melt like wax around him. I can't say no to him.

Looking past him, I see August still passed out on the couch, where I'm sure he'll be for the rest of the night. Moving my gaze back to Logan's, I nod slowly. "Okay..."

He doesn't let go of my wrist, instead he slides his hand down to mine, lacing his fingers between mine as I step into my bedroom. Logan follows me and I let go of his hand as he walks past me and I shut the door behind us. The lock turns effortlessly as I secure it, just in case.

As I turn around, I see Logan sitting on the edge of my bed with his head in his hands. I freeze for a moment, my chest constricting as I see how broken he looks too. My feet move without my direction and don't stop until I'm standing directly in front of him, reaching for his wrists. Pulling his hands away from his face, he lifts his head, his blue eyes wet as they find mine.

"What did you want to talk about, Logan?"

His eyes search mine. "Are you and Silas a thing?"

I'm taken aback by his question, my brow furrowing. "No. Why would you even suggest that?"

"I've seen the two of you together. You're always

together. And then you left with him today after school."

I stare down at him, my hands still wrapped around his wrists. My heart races in my chest, beating erratically against its cage. "Have you been watching me, Logan?"

He shrugs without any shame, probably given his drunken state. "So what if I have been? If I can't have you, no one else can."

"Well, that's some fucked-up logic." I laugh lightly as he pulls his wrists from my grip. He reaches for me, wrapping his hands around the backs of my thighs as he pulls me closer to him. "You know, no one said you can't have me, Logan."

"Baby, baby, baby," he murmurs softly, wrapping his arms around me as he presses the side of his face to my stomach. My hands instinctively find his head and I stroke his soft hair as he holds me close. "You know it's not that simple, right?"

"Why can't we just tell August?"

Logan sighs, nuzzling his head against my abdomen. "I want to. I just don't know how to."

Grabbing the sides of his head, I pull him away from my body and tilt his head back to meet his eyes. "We can figure it out together, okay?" I pause for a moment. "You're drunk, though, so how am I supposed to know that tomorrow morning you're not going to change your mind?"

His lips curve upward and he shakes his head. "I'm not that drunk, baby. Trust me, when it comes to you, there's no amount of alcohol that could ever make me forget a moment with you." He pauses, his tongue darting out to lick his lips. "But really, I didn't drink that much, I promise."

Without warning, he falls backward onto my bed, landing on his back as he pulls me along with him. It catches me off guard and I yelp as I crash down onto his chest before we both begin to laugh. "You asshole," I giggle, pushing my hands against his firm pecs.

Logan stops laughing, his hands sliding up my torso and to the sides of my neck before he cups the sides of my face. A fire dances in his eyes as I meet his smoldering gaze and my breath catches in my throat. "I really want to fucking kiss you right now," he murmurs, pulling my face closer to his. "Can I kiss you, baby?"

I swallow hard over the knives in my throat and nod. A smile forms on his lips before they meet mine. His mouth is soft and tender, his tongue darting out as he traces the seam and parts my lips. I open for him, letting him in as he steals the air from my lungs in one swift movement. His tongue slides against mine, caught in a slow dance as it tangles with mine.

Logan rolls me over onto my back, moving with me without his mouth leaving mine as he positions himself on top of me. I'm lost in him, my hands sliding up his back, under his shirt as he slides his fingers along my scalp, diving into my hair. He kisses me slowly and it's a painful torture as he takes his time.

His cock is hard, pressing against me as he settles between my legs. He deepens the kiss, draining my lungs of oxygen and my head begins to swim from the deprivation. When it comes down to it, this is all I want with him. To feel him close, knowing I'm the only one who occupies his mind. And right now, in this moment, I know I want more with him.

My hands find his shoulders and I push him away, coming up for air as our mouths break apart. Panic fills his eyes as they rapidly search mine, as if he did something wrong. "Take your clothes off," I tell him, the lust heavy in my words. "I want more, Logan. From you... only you."

"Are you sure, baby girl?" His voice is soft and tender, just like his hands as he slides them along my torso. "I don't want you to feel pressured to do something you don't want to do."

"I've never been more sure in my entire life," I tell him honestly, as I move my hands with his, pushing my shirt up higher.

Logan moves away from me, standing up beside my bed as he pulls his shirt over his head and tosses it onto the floor. I sit up with him, following suit as I take off my own shirt. He stands there silently, a fire burning in his eyes as he watches me slowly take my bra off and drop it onto the floor. The flames burn brighter as his gaze roams across my body.

As I reach for the waistband of my pants, Logan covers my hands with his and pulls them away. "Let me do it," he whispers, dropping to his knees on the floor in front of me. He's gentle as he slides my pants and underwear down my thighs, leaving me naked on the bed in front of him. "Goddamn, you're fucking beautiful."

A heat crawls up my neck, spreading across my cheeks as I feel his gaze traveling across my body. This is the first time I've ever been naked in front of anyone, but I don't feel embarrassed like I thought I would. Instead, he makes me feel like I'm the most beautiful thing he's ever seen.

He doesn't move from where he's kneeling on

the floor as he places his hands on my knees and slowly parts them. Logan inches closer, his fingertips digging into my flesh as his palms warm my skin. "I wanna taste you, baby," he murmurs, his heated gaze finding mine. "Has anyone ever tasted you before?"

Swallowing roughly, I shake my head. "No," I whisper, not fully trusting my voice as a warmth spreads through my lower abdomen. "I want you to be my first."

The corners of Logan's lips lift. "And your last, Isla. I'm going to ruin you for anyone else. I'm going to leave my mark so deep in your fucking soul that you won't ever want anyone but me."

"I never have."

"Good girl," he murmurs, his face inching closer to the apex of my thighs. His eyes burn holes through mine as he stares straight into my soul. "Lay back for me, pretty girl. Let me taste this sweet pussy and make you feel good."

Lowering myself back onto my bed, his warm breath skates across my skin before he presses his lips along the inside of my thighs. Holding my legs apart with his hands, he trails his mouth up both sides of my legs before he reaches my center. His lips are warm as he gently presses them against my pussy. My hips buck and my hands reach for him, gripping his hair as he drags his tongue along me.

"Fuck," he breathes against me, nipping at my clit before sucking it into his mouth. My eyes roll back into my head as he tastes me, teasing me with his tongue. It's unlike anything I've ever felt before and I don't want this feeling to ever end.

"Don't stop," I breathe, writhing as he works his tongue against me, fucking me with his mouth.

He lifts his head for a moment, a smile tugging on the corners of his lips.

"I'm not stopping until you come on my tongue, baby."

A warmth spreads through the pit of my stomach as Logan continues to taste and tease me with his tongue. My eyes fall shut as a wave of ecstasy washes over me and I'm seeing goddamn stars from the way he flicks my clit. I'm so close to falling over the edge and he's not stopping until I'm plummeting.

He slides a finger inside me, pumping it in and out as he draws my clit back into my mouth, rolling his tongue over the bundle of nerves. With one more thrust of his hand, a swipe of his tongue, and he's shoving me off a cliff. My orgasm racks my body with such force, I'm a goddamn mess, crying out as an earthquake erupts inside me.

Logan pulls away as I ride out the lasting waves of my orgasm, a smirk forming on his face as he crawls up my body. "So sweet and so fucking innocent," he murmurs, his lips finding mine with the taste of me on his tongue. "I'm so gone for you, baby girl."

CHAPTER EIGHTEEN
LOGAN

Isla slides her hands down my torso, her fingers finding the waistband of my pants as she slides them beneath it. My breath catches in my throat and her hands are hesitant as she begins to push my pants down farther. Pulling away from her, I brace myself on my hands beside her head, my eyes searching hers.

"Are you sure, Isla?" I question her, and she nods. "I don't want you to feel pressured into doing something that you're not ready for."

"I want this." Her voice is tender and quiet as she stares directly into my soul. "I'm ready, Logan, I promise."

Pushing away from the bed, I slowly rise to my feet and Isla follows, sitting up as I stand in front of her. Her eyes are on mine, slowly trailing down my torso as I hook my fingers under the waistband of my pants, sliding them underneath my boxers as I slide them down my thighs and my calves.

I watch her face transform as she scans my body, her eyes wide as she stops at my erection that is currently throbbing between my legs. Her throat bobs as she swallows hard before meeting my gaze. I've never felt self-conscious or nervous before, but under her watchful eye, I've never felt more exposed.

"There's no way that's going to fit," she blurts out, her cheeks turning pink as she drops her gaze back to my cock. "Logan. I don't think this is going to work."

A chuckle rumbles in my throat as I step closer to her, my hands cupping the sides of her face as I tilt her head back. "I promise you that we can make it fit, baby girl."

She swallows hard again, her eyes searching mine, but something else washes over her gaze. Trust. She's giving me that—to keep her safe, to protect her.

"I can't promise you it won't hurt or be uncomfortable at first..."

Isla grabs my wrists, pulling my hands away

from her face as she continues to stare up at me. She wraps her delicate hand around the base of my cock, squeezing it lightly as she licks her lips. "I don't know what I'm doing," she admits quietly and I swear to God, I'm about to fucking blow.

"There's nothing you can do wrong."

She opens her mouth, bringing it to the tip of my cock as she slowly slides the head along her tongue. Her hand grips the base and she's hesitant as she slides the shaft deeper into her mouth. Her eyes flutter open and she stares up at me with my cock pressed between her pretty lips.

I sharply inhale, my hand finding the back of her head as she moves her hand in tandem with her mouth. "That's it, baby. You're doing fucking amazing."

Her eyes shine back at me before her eyelids flutter shut. With one hand gripping my cock and her lips wrapped around the tip, she bobs her head back and forth, drawing me in and out of her mouth in rapid succession. There's a part of me that almost doesn't believe she's never done this before, because fuck...

A warmth spreads through the pit of my stomach and I know I need her to stop now before I end up losing myself inside her mouth. Both of my hands find the sides of her head and I pull her away from me. She's still sitting on the bed, me standing in front of her, so I lightly push her back, lowering her down onto the bed as I follow after her.

"What's wrong?" she asks, the panic evident in her voice as her eyes search mine.

Planting my hands on the bed, I hover above her as I settle between her legs. "Nothing at all, babe." A low chuckle vibrates in my chest. "Quite the opposite. If you didn't stop, it would have been game over."

A pink tint creeps across her cheeks and she smiles at me innocently. The tip of my cock presses against her center and I pause for a moment, watching as her face transforms and her eyes widen.

"Shit," I mutter, shaking my head. "I need to grab a condom."

Just as I'm about to move away from her, Isla hooks her ankles around the back of my waist. "Don't go," she breathes, her eyes burning a hole through mine. "I'm on the pill…"

Fuck…

My already hard cock aches and I stare back down at her, searching her eyes for confirmation that this is really what she wants. Isla nods, linking her hands around the back of my neck as she brings my face down to hers. Our mouths collide and I inhale her, breathing her in as our tongues tangle together.

The head of my cock presses against her and I feel her tense, her body falling rigid out of it being unfamiliar. "Relax for me, baby girl," I murmur against her lips, drawing the bottom one into my mouth as I nip at it.

Isla moans in my mouth and I swallow her sounds, her body relaxing beneath me as I slowly push into her. She doesn't try to fight me, but fuck, she's so goddamn tight. I know it's hurting her as she winces beneath me, her lips slowing against mine.

"Do you want me to stop?" I whisper as I pull back to look at her.

Isla shakes her head, pulling me closer with her legs as I fully enter her in one swift movement. Her lips part slightly, a ragged breath slipping from her, and her eyes widen as I fill her to the brim. "Oh my god," she breathes, her face contorting in pleasure and pain.

My movements are slow as I draw my hips back, my cock sliding out slightly before thrusting back into her. I attempt to take my time, to be gentle and tender, but it's taking every ounce of self-control to not fuck her into oblivion in this goddamn moment.

Her pussy is so tight—so wet—and she clenches around me like a fucking vise grip. "Don't stop, Logan," she breathes, panting as I thrust into her again and again. She pulls me back down to her, our mouths colliding as I swallow her moans.

I work against her, stretching her out as I continue to slide my hips back and forth. I don't want to hurt her, but she's more relaxed, like she's more comfortable and enjoying it. If she weren't, she wouldn't be moaning my name and clawing at my back, begging me not to stop.

Moving one hand, I reach down between us, finding her clit with the tips of my fingers. Applying pressure, I play with her, rolling the sensitive flesh under my fingertips as I continue to fuck her. Isla's quickly coming undone, writhing under my touch as I push her closer and closer to the edge.

My balls constrict, drawing closer to my body as the warmth in the pit of my stomach begins to spread. "I'm going to come, baby girl."

"Come with me," she breathes against my lips. "I'm right there."

Rolling my fingers over her clit once more, I slam

my hips into her, my cock filling her deeply as she cries out in ecstasy. "Come *for* me."

That's all it takes to send her plummeting over the edge, straight into the euphoric abyss. Her body shakes, her legs quivering as she tightens them around me. Her pussy clamps down, squeezing the fucking life out of my cock as her orgasm rocks her body, straight to her core. It takes everything in me to let her ride out the waves of ecstasy before pulling out of her.

I almost don't make it out, the cum spurting from my cock just as I'm pulling out of her pulsating pussy. My lips part slightly, a ragged breath slipping from my lips as my chest rises and falls in rapid succession. I'm completely captivated, watching her spread out for me as I coat her pussy with my come.

"So fucking beautiful," I murmur, my eyes traveling up her body to hers. Fully satiated and glazed over from the high she's still riding.

"And so fucking mine…"

CHAPTER NINETEEN
ISLA

"What are you doing tonight?" Silas questions me as we walk out of class, falling in step with the crowd of students that fill the hallway. I see Octavia and Demi waiting for us at the top of the stairs. "We were all talking about going bowling or something."

I glance at Silas as we make our way toward the two of them. "I think that I'm just going to stay in tonight."

As we reach Demi and Octavia, they both greet us, Octavia's eyes meeting Silas's. "Did you tell her what we were planning on doing tonight?"

Silas nods, frowning as he glances at me, motioning for me to tell her the same thing I told him. As I tell her that I plan on just staying at home, she gives me a look of disapproval. "See," Silas tells her as we all head down the stairs and into the corridor of the building. "I tried to get her to come."

"Sorry, guys," I tell them, shrugging as I offer a small smile. "I really just don't feel like going out at all."

We walk through the front doors and I notice Logan's car pulled up along the curb as he sits and waits for me. Octavia glances at me, raising her eyebrows as she bumps her shoulder into mine. "It wouldn't have anything to do with a certain hot hockey player that lives with you, would it?"

I look over at her, a laugh bubbling out of me, but it sounds forced and nervous. Silas narrows his eyes before glaring at Logan through the tinted windows. "No." I shake my head at the three of them. "I have a lot of studying I need to get done."

Demi and Silas fall into conversation as they turn to the right and continue walking down the sidewalk. Octavia walks closer to Logan's car with me, pausing as I reach for the door.

"If you decide to change your mind, call me," she smiles, winking at me before jogging off after Silas and Demi.

I pull open the car door and slide inside as Logan lowers the volume of the music and turns to look at me. He has on a black t-shirt that hugs his firm body, leading down to a pair of gray joggers. My eyes trail back up to his, and he smirks at me.

"What?" I question him, turning away as I reach for my seat belt, feeling the heat creeping up my neck and spreading across my cheeks. I've spent the past decade admiring him from afar. Now, I feel like I'm allowed to do it when we're in private without being judged—although he seems like he's eating this up.

"Oh, nothing." He directs his attention to the car as he puts it in drive and pulls away from the front of the building. "I'm happy to see you, too."

We've fallen into this comfortable routine over the past month. I never intended on having sex with him that night, but it's like it opened a new door to whatever this is between us. We had both agreed that we needed to come clean with my brother, but for some reason, it never felt like the right time. I know Logan is afraid of losing his best friend and the last thing I want to do is tear them apart.

Logan plays it off like he has other things to do, but in reality, he sneaks into my room after August goes to bed. In a way, it's like we're back in the past, sneaking around, but there's so much more at stake now. This is different from drunken kisses and secretive touches... we're playing with a deck of 52 hearts.

I just wonder how long until one of us folds...

———

When we get to the apartment, August is already there, freshly showered and pacing the kitchen. He pauses, glancing at the two of us as we enter, but he doesn't say anything because he still doesn't suspect anything even though it's literally right in front of his face.

There's a part of me that wishes he would find out on his own, but I don't think that would be for the best. He trusts Logan and if that were to be broken, I don't know whether their friendship would ever recover from that. My brother might be a clown and mess around, but when it comes to loyalty, that is everything to him.

"What are you doing?" I ask him as I drop my bag onto the floor and sit down at the dining room table. "You look like you need me to call that therapist Mom had you see in high school."

"Fuck you." He cuts his eyes at me before rolling them. "That was a weird time in my life and I told you I never want to talk about that shit again."

Logan looks back and forth between the two of us before grabbing a bottle of water from the fridge. As he bends to lean forward, his shirt rides up a bit and my eyes travel along the skin that shows, wishing he would just take it off. "You know, there's nothing to be ashamed of for going to therapy. It's not that big of a deal, Whitley."

August crosses his arms defensively over his chest. "Dude. Having night terrors as a teenager is embarrassing as hell. It would be one thing if I went through something traumatic or had a good reasoning behind it. The only thing they found out was that I had a fucking sleeping disorder."

Logan looks at me as August begins to pace again, mumbling under his breath. My brother is usually a carefree person, one who isn't really affected by things, but when something does bother him, it really messes with him. One thing he had always struggled with was his ability to regulate his emotions. He might not show it to everyone else, but August is actually quite sensitive and his feelings are big.

This isn't unusual for Logan to see, but I don't know if he ever knew about the whole sleeping issue. I'm sure he was at our house once or twice when August had a night terror, but when he was experiencing the worst of it, he actually distanced himself from his friends and didn't sleep anywhere else or have anyone sleep at our house.

So, even though Logan isn't new to August and his emotions, I'm wondering how much August has really shared with his best friend.

"August." My voice is stern and firm as I rise to my feet and walk into the kitchen. Logan moves out of my way, stepping into the doorway as he leans back and props himself against it. August stops moving, his eyes finding mine as he lets out a ragged breath. "Tell me what is going on."

"Fuck," he mutters, pressing back against the cabinets before sinking onto the floor. He drops down, propping his back against the door, and I sit down with him. There's something about being on the floor that always helps August get back to where he needs to be mentally. "Okay," he breathes, inhaling deeply before he lets out a ragged breath. "I went to the bar after class to talk to Poppy, but I found out that she quit."

"Okay..." my voice trails off, my head tilting to the side as I attempt to figure out where he's going with this. I'm not sure what is really going on here and he hasn't gotten to the root of it yet. "Did you try calling her?"

"Yeah." His voice is quiet—off—and distant. "She had her number disconnected. I went to her apartment and it was empty."

Reaching out, I grab his forearm and give it a light squeeze. "Why this sudden change of wanting to talk to her? You haven't talked much about her since you found out she had a new boyfriend last month."

"So, it all seemed weird to me, right?" His eyes focus on mine as a wave of suspicion passes through his troubled gaze. "You know, we were kind of seeing each other. And then boom, she has a boyfriend. At the time, I didn't really question it, because whatever, she's an adult and can do whatever she wants."

Logan steps forward, dropping down onto the floor with us as he takes a seat beside August. "It wasn't her boyfriend, was it?"

August looks over at him, shaking his head. "I asked Amanda when she told me that Poppy quit and she had no idea what I was talking about." He glances back at me. "Turns out, her car had broken down and that was her cousin that picked her up. She tried to play it off like it was something it wasn't."

"Did Amanda know anything you didn't?"

He shakes his head, sighing. "Other than what she told me, no. They weren't really close enough that Poppy confided in her. I just can't get it out of my head. Something had to have happened that made her lie to me, and then she just disappeared... I don't know what to do."

"I don't think you really can do anything, August," Logan offers quietly, his eyes on the side of August's face. "How are you supposed to find her if she changed her phone number? Maybe she had to leave for a family emergency. I don't know, man."

August abruptly climbs to his feet, shaking his head dismissively at Logan. "No, this is weird and I need to know what happened." He pauses, glancing at me. "I'm going to go take a nap and try to get rid of this headache. Don't bother me for dinner."

A frown forms on my face as I watch him disappear from the room. Whenever August gets beside himself like this, it's almost as if his brain can't handle it. He typically gets bad headaches when he can't control his emotions and the only solution is sleeping. It hurts my heart, seeing him like this and knowing that I can't do anything for my brother.

"He'll be okay," Logan tells me as he slowly stands up and puts his hand out for me. His palm is warm as I slide my hand in his and he helps me to my feet. "He just needs some time to process that she really left without giving him an explanation."

My eyes search Logan's as I stand in front of him, my hand still in his. "You really think that he'll let it go at that and not obsess over it?"

Logan shrugs. "I think he might have to." He turns his back slightly, but he doesn't let my hand go as he leads me from the kitchen. I glance toward the hallway where August went into his room and check to make sure that he doesn't see me holding his best friends hand. "Let's just order take-out and watch movies."

He grabs the remote and flops down on the couch. Putting some space between us, I sit two cushions away from him, pulling my feet up as I tuck my legs underneath me and curl into the plush cushions. "As long as it isn't anything scary."

"I know. You've never been a fan of anything horror-related." A playful smirk plays on his lips as his eyes shine at me. "What if I told you I would never let anything happen to you? That I would always keep you safe?"

Grabbing the pillow beside me, I laugh lightly and throw it at him as I shake my head. "Nope. You're not going to convince me to watch anything that will give me nightmares with empty promises like that."

Logan narrows his eyes slightly. "They're not empty promises, baby." His voice is low and soft and the oceanic depths of his eyes are warm. "One day, I'll make you see."

Swallowing roughly over the lump in my throat, I stare back at him as he stares straight into my soul. I don't know what to believe with Logan because he confuses me more than anything else. Whatever this is between us is a conundrum and he's a contradiction. How will he make me see if we're always going to be a secret?

"Well, isn't this cute?" August's voice breaks through the silence as he strolls into the living room with his pillow. "I can't sleep right now. What are you love birds doing?"

My heart stops and my chest constricts as my body kicks into manual breathing, and my brain suddenly forgets how the hell to do it. Logan's gaze lands on August as he drops down onto the chaise lounge and sprawls out. I widen my eyes as I stare at the TV, praying the couch will swallow me whole.

"I'm fucking with you. That would be like incest, since I know she's like a sister to you too," August says slowly, his words drawn out as he narrows his eyes at us both. I don't meet his gaze, but I can feel it on the side of my head. "Unless I should be worried about something?"

This is the chance we've both been waiting for—the moment we can officially break the ice and come clean with August. My lips part slightly, the words on the tip of my tongue, but Logan interjects before I get a chance to speak.

"Absolutely not." Logan's voice is controlled and calm, like he has rehearsed this a million times. My heart sinks and my lungs deflate as my hopes come crashing down. "You're nuts for even insinuating that. You have nothing to worry about, trust me."

As if his first admission wasn't like a slap to the face, I can barely stomach his last two sentences. I look over at August, whose eyes find mine, needing confirmation that Logan is telling the truth. This is my chance, but I can't do that to Logan. I won't ruin their friendship.

"He's right, August." I smile at him, rolling my eyes for good measure. "I'm not stupid enough to get involved with someone like him."

August grabs the remote from Logan as he settles on his back on the couch and flips through the channels. "Good," he mumbles, staring at the TV as Logan's eyes find mine. "Because I'm pretty sure I'd fucking kill you."

A shadow passes over Logan's face as his eyes desperately search mine. He wants to know if what I said was true—if I meant what I said. Turning away from him, I don't give him the satisfaction as I settle deeper into the cushions and ignore him.

That's the problem with the two of us.

We're both fucking liars.

CHAPTER TWENTY
LOGAN

I don't know what the hell my problem is.

No matter what I try to do, I can't manage to stop fucking this up between Isla and I. I know I'm being a real piece of shit, going behind my best friend's back and fucking around with his little sister. He'll never forgive me when he knows the truth, but I need to grow some balls and tell him already. Even if it means that he kills me, at least it would be better than this guilty feeling of deceiving him.

It's all my fault.

I fucked around and got attached. And now that I've had her in my arms, I'm not letting her go again.

I just need to find the right time to tell August and after last night, I know that Isla wasn't happy with the way I responded to him. I should have come clean in that moment, but I panicked and I covered it all up, which I know made her feel like shit. Her little comment didn't make me feel any better, but I deserved it.

She deserves better.

And August deserves the truth.

Cam walks over to me as he pulls his t-shirt over his head. We just finished practice and I successfully got my ass handed to me. That's what I get for being distracted. I fucked up during our drills and our coach made me pay for it in sweat and energy.

"You wanna come with us to get some beers?" Cam asks as he drops down onto the bench beside me. I finish shoving my stuff into my hockey bag before turning to look at him.

"Nah." I shrug and shake my head as I rise to my feet. "I'm going to go home and get a real shower and probably lay low."

"Since when did you become such a buzzkill?" He snorts, crossing his arms over his chest. "You used to be fun and now it seems like you never want to hang out with the guys anymore."

Cam's confession hits me in the chest like a ton of bricks. He's right. That's the thing about being a part of a team—it's almost like a brotherhood.

These guys have become family and if he feels like I've been neglecting them, who knows how the rest of them are feeling. August hasn't said anything, but he wouldn't. He would rather them approach me than get caught in the middle.

"Since he started fucking someone on the low that he refuses to disclose," August interjects as he rounds the corner and stops in front of us. "Isn't that right, Knight?"

Grabbing the handle of my bag, I narrow my eyes at him. "Actually, no, that's not right."

"Hmm," he muses, dropping down beside Cam as he tilts his head to the side. "So, where have you been sneaking off to in the middle of the night?"

Oh, fuck... he knows.

Cam looks up at me with curiosity. "What? Okay, this is all making sense now."

I need to cover this up. If August has noticed my absence, then he knows there is something going on. He just doesn't know with whom, and given the current situation, I don't know if it's best that I drop this bomb on him.

"There really isn't." I glue my eyes to August's. "Since you have to be such an asshole about it, I've been having trouble sleeping since I found out that my father wanted to talk."

It wasn't entirely a lie. I still haven't decided if I want to talk to him or not yet, but it's the only excuse I can come up with right now to get August off my back. The way his face falls instantly makes me feel guilty and I can't back down now.

"Shit," he murmurs, hanging his head as Cam purses his lips. "I am an asshole."

I shake my head in an attempt to make him not feel as guilty, when it's really me who should be feeling like shit. Just add this to the list of deceitful things I've been doing to my best friend and another reason why he's never going to speak to me again when the truth finally comes out.

"Look," Cam interjects into our moment, his deep green eyes bouncing back and forth between the two of us. "I know you said you don't want to go out with us and would rather just go home, but maybe it would be good for you. Like old times. Come hang out with all of us and you can maybe clear your head of all of this shit."

August looks at me with a glimmer of hope in his eyes. I know Cam is right, but it's like I'm being torn into two different directions. I want to go home and find Isla. I need to talk to her, to explain once again and attempt to beg for her forgiveness and understanding. But on the other hand, I need time with the boys. It's been too long and it's clear that they're feeling my absence.

"You're right," I tell both of them as I roll my bag back into the center of the locker room. "Let me just grab a shower here, then and I'll go with you guys."

"Yes!" Cam fist pumps, acting like a little kid who is high on a sugar rush. "It's been too long. Finally, all the boys are going to be back together."

August laughs, shoving Cam away as he attempts to hug both of our shoulders and pull us together. "Damn, Logan. You smell like you haven't washed yourself in weeks."

"I mean, Coach did just ride him harder than anyone else tonight," August offers as he pulls out his phone. He absentmindedly scrolls, no doubt attempting to find something about Poppy again. After last night, he kind of settled with the entire thing, but I know that his mind works against him and he's probably still thinking about her.

He needs this distraction as much as I do.

"Fuck you both," I say, giving them the middle finger as I grab a clean change of clothes from my bag and head to the shower. "If you guys wanna head out now, I'll just meet you wherever you end up."

Cam stands up as August nods. "I'll go talk to

the other guys and August will text you where we'll be at." Cam pauses for a moment, narrowing his eyes at me. "You better not bitch out."

August crosses his arms over his chest and I feel like I'm being scolded by my parents right now with the way they're both looking at me. "Logan knows better. He'll show up."

Rolling my eyes, I head toward the showers and slip inside one of the stalls. As I strip out of my clothes, I pull my phone from my pocket and open up my text messages. Of course there's nothing from Isla, but that doesn't mean I'm going to leave her alone.

LOGAN

> Hey you. Are you going to be home later?

I fold up my clothes and set them on the bench, leaving the message thread open. I watch as the three little dots pop up a few times, each time disappearing as if she's not sure how to respond or she's choosing her words carefully. Turning away from it, I turn on the shower and let the water heat up before stepping into it.

As I'm putting some shampoo on my hands, my phone dings as a text message comes through. I quickly run the soap through my hair and scrub my scalp before rinsing it out. I grab a towel and dry my hands before grabbing my phone in haste, my eyes desperately needing to read something from Isla.

> ISLA
>
> I don't know yet. Octavia invited me to a party, so I might go out with her.

My jaw clenches. I don't want her to isolate herself from her friends, except for the one. The one who always seems to get in the fucking way and who wants what is mine.

> LOGAN
>
> Is Silas going to be there?

> ISLA
>
> Maybe? Does it really matter?

This girl. Of course it matters. I can see why she would think it might not matter to me after last night, but we were both in the wrong. Hell, we've both been in the wrong since she moved into our apartment. We just need to come together and figure out a way to rectify the situation together.

LOGAN

We need to talk.

I watch the bubbles do the same thing, appearing and then disappearing. I wait for a moment, but they don't come back, almost as if she chose not to respond. A frustrated sigh slips from my lips and my heart pounds erratically in my chest.

Stepping back into the hot water, I grab my washcloth and begin to scrub the sweat from practice from my skin. In this moment, I really regret agreeing to go out with the guys. As much as I want to see them and spend some time with them, I need to talk to Isla. I need things to be okay between us.

I finish washing my body and turn off the shower, with still no response from Isla. I didn't expect to get this attached to her, even though it was something that had been happening since we were kids. I never really imagined my life without her in it and after I went away to college and had a taste of life without her, I didn't want that.

I never fully wanted that, but I wanted to give her a chance to find someone else. I should have given her the same chance when she got here. Just because we were living together didn't mean she had to be with me, but I already knew I couldn't be without her, especially having her be so close to me.

But now that we're in this deep, there's no backing out. There's no exit or escape route. The only thing we can do is cling to each other as we head straight into the flames of our destruction. I never promised her this would end well, but with whatever happens, I will always keep her safe.

So, when I tell her brother tonight, I will make sure Isla makes it out unscathed.

She isn't the villain of this story.

I am.

CHAPTER TWENTY-ONE
ISLA

"It's about time you come back out with us!" Octavia yells out to me as we head into the house, the bass from the music almost drowning out her voice. I follow after her through the sea of people as we head into the kitchen.

She wraps her long fingers around a bottle of vodka and pours it into two plastic cups as I grab some orange juice sitting on the counter with a bunch of different mixers. Octavia pours them in with the liquor and hands me one with a bright smile on her face.

"Seriously, girl. As much as I love Demi, I've missed you." She taps her cup against mine and we both swallow a mouthful before she smiles at me again. My throat burns as the vodka slides down into my stomach and I welcome the warmth, knowing this is going to get me exactly where I need to be tonight. As mentally distant from Logan as possible.

I never did respond to his message and left him on read, even though I knew it would make his blood boil. He deserved to just sit with that and stew on it for a little. It wasn't fair, this game we've been playing. All it's doing is muddling our minds and I don't like it.

At first, there was a certain degree of excitement, sneaking around. That was a long time ago and we're past that now. I'm tired of being his secret and I'm tired of feeling like what we are doing is shameful. Sure, my brother might not agree with it, but when it comes down to it, it really isn't his decision. It's completely out of his control.

Logan and I are both consenting adults who can make their own decisions. Neither of us planned for this to happen, to fall so goddamn deep down this hole together, but now we're here, there's no way out.

And when I finally give Logan the chance to talk, I'm going to tell him how this is going to go. He has a choice he needs to make. Either we tell my brother about us or this stops now.

I'm tired of playing this endless game with Logan.

It's all or nothing.

I'm well on my way to drunk as I dance with Octavia. Demi showed up at some point, but she disappeared with Mace, Silas's friend. Neither of us questioned her on it because she's had her eyes on him for a while, always pestering Silas about getting Mace's number. I don't know how it happened between them, but it looks like she finally got what she wanted.

Octavia is pretty drunk already. She bounces around, her body swaying with the music as she holds her hands above her head. Some random guy steps behind her, his hands finding her waist. She opens her eyes and they find mine as her lips curl upward into a smirk. Instead of pushing the guy away, she grinds her hips.

I laugh, shaking my head at her as she spins around and wraps her arms around the guy's neck. They dance together and I suddenly feel like I'm a third wheel, even though this guy came out of nowhere. I'm not sure what his name is, but I've seen him around campus. Either way, good for Octavia.

Honestly, I'm kind of glad she has someone to distract her right now so she can keep her nose out of my business. She's been bothering me more and more about what's going on between Logan and I and I keep having to plead the fifth, even though she knows there's something going on.

It's exhausting, trying to keep up this charade of secrecy. I can't risk anyone knowing the truth because if someone knows, then it's only a matter of time before August finds out. And if he finds out from someone other than Logan or me, it's not going to end well.

I drain the rest of my drink from my cup and make my way through the crowd that moves their sweaty bodies together to the beat of the music. No one seems to mind as I push past them and finally make my way through the clearing and into the kitchen. I grab a bottle of vodka and more orange juice as I make another drink.

Standing facing the counter, I lift the cup to my mouth when I feel a pair of hands sliding along my waist. It catches me off guard, taking me by surprise as I jump and yelp. The warmth of his breath skates along my ear as he laughs lightly, spinning me around in his grip.

It's not who I want it to be, though.

Silas's gaze meets mine, his lips tipping upward as he stares down at me. "I've been looking for you."

"Well, I've been here all night," I offer, smiling back at him as I try to rein myself back. There's a bluish tint to the greens of Silas's irises that I've never noticed before. He's attractive, with his symmetrical features and chiseled jaw. I've tried to not look at him as more than a friend, but right now, he looks like a bad decision and I find myself leaning into him.

Get it together, Isla. Just because I'm drunk doesn't mean I need to go making some impulsive decision.

"When did you get here?" I ask him, taking a step back from his grasp. His face falls for a moment, but he quickly recovers as he makes himself a drink.

"Maybe like a half hour ago," he replies with a shrug. I watch the column of his throat bob as he swallows a mouthful of the liquor in his cup. "I lied when I said I've been looking for you. I saw you dancing with Octavia when I got here."

My eyebrows draw together as my eyes bounce

back and forth between his. "So, why didn't you come over to us?"

He stares at me with a heated gaze, his fingers soft against my face as he brushes a stray hair behind my ear. "Because I liked watching you."

I swallow roughly over the panic that is building inside me. It's suddenly too hot in here and it feels as if the walls are closing in on me. I feel claustrophobic as fuck and I can't tell if it's because I'm too drunk or because Silas is coming on to me.

And the fact that my mind is working against me, telling me to do something I'm inevitably going to regret.

"Can we go outside?" I ask him, taking a step away from him, my body swaying from the alcohol racing through my system. "It's really hot and loud in here."

Silas nods, stepping toward me as he wraps his arm around my waist. "Of course, babe. Let's go outside, somewhere where it's more quiet... more private."

My heart screams at me to go back inside, but my mind tells it to fuck off as I let Silas take me out onto the back patio. This is what Logan does to me. He fucks with my head so much that I don't know what is up or down. I need to forget him, to forget the way that he makes me feel.

I lied when I said there was no way out of this hole we've fallen down together.

There's only one way out and it ends with both of our hearts in shattered fragments.

CHAPTER TWENTY-TWO
LOGAN

"It was nice finally hanging out again." Cam slurs his words as we all make our way out into the parking lot to our cars. Thankfully he rode here with Sterling, who isn't nearly as drunk as him so he's better off driving.

"I know," I tell him, his bloodshot eyes searching mine. "You guys are my family and I've just been losing sight of a lot of shit lately. I needed this, to remind me of what's important. And I'll be more present."

Cam pulls me in for a hug as he sways slightly. He pats my back before releasing me. "We won't let you disappear like that again. Don't forget, we're your brothers. You got some shit going on and we got your back, always."

"Thanks, bro," I smile as he stumbles toward the car. I glance at Sterling, who shakes his head at our sloppy friend. "Make sure he sleeps that shit off."

Sterling nods, before climbing into his car. I step away, making my way over to mine that is parked beside August's. He lingers along the driver's-side door of his car.

"I talked to Isla earlier," he says, with nothing in his voice that indicates he knows I was talking to her too. "She told me about some party she was going to tonight. I tried texting her before we left the bar but she didn't respond. I was going to head over there and see what's good."

She never responded to me, but she did to him and told him exactly where she was going to be. I don't know whether I need to be checking up on her like this, but I told her I wanted to talk tonight. And if she's not home, then there's no talking to her.

"Were you going there to check on her or because you're not ready to go home?"

August smirks. "If I'm at home alone, it's too quiet and my mind is too loud. So, I don't know. I don't want to go home, but I should probably make sure she's okay too."

I weigh my options carefully before speaking. "I'll ride with you."

"Good," August nods as I walk over to his car. "You can drive my car home from the party then, because I don't want to get in any sort of trouble if I end up drinking while we're there."

We leave the bar together and I can't help but feel like this is the time I should talk to him. Although, he's been a little mentally unstable lately and with him behind the wheel... I'm afraid for my life if I say the wrong thing and piss him off.

I need to talk to Isla first. She needs to know about the explosion and be able to anticipate the shrapnel before I drop that bomb on him.

When we get to the party, the thing is already in full swing. Some girl stands out in the flower bed, puking into the snow as we walk up into the house. A few other people were out there with her, so neither of us were too concerned walking past her. Plus, at this time of night, it's not something unusual or surprising to see.

We wade through the crowd and I follow after August. I spot her friend—Octavia, I think—as she walks into the kitchen at the same time as us. I nudge August, nodding toward her as he catches my eye.

"Hey, is Isla still here?" he asks her as she stumbles into the counter with some guy reaching for her waist.

Octavia giggles, her bloodshot eyes meeting August's. "Yeah, she's here. I think I saw her with Silas a little while ago."

The mention of his name has my blood instantly boiling. My breath catches in my throat and my hands curl into fists by my side. I'm not drunk, by any means, but my body felt warm from the beers I had at the bar. That feeling quickly dissipates as I feel my body grow cold. Fuck this.

August thanks her, but I'm already brushing past him, heading through the house. I feel his hand as he grabs my shoulder, pulling me back. "Dude, chill out. Octavia said she's still here, so she's fine. I'm sure we'll find her somewhere, but I'm going to get a drink quick."

I look back at him, shrugging his hand from my shoulder as I nod. He turns his back to me, heading over to where all the alcohol is, and I take this as my chance to duck out of the room. August doesn't see me as I dip out through the doorway and I don't need him to follow after me. He might not be worried about Isla, but I am. Especially knowing she's with Silas.

I make my way through the house and it's

almost like a replay of the last party I found her at. She's nowhere to be found so I quickly exit out the back door and out onto the back patio. I've seen the way Silas looks at her; I know exactly what he wants from her, because I want it too. There's no doubt in my mind he tried to get her somewhere dark and quiet, away from everyone else.

As I make my way through the small groups of people hovering around one another, I see them toward the back of the yard, sitting on a wooden bench swing together. My feet carry me across the yard, through the snow as I tromp toward them. Silas has his arm around the back of her shoulders, both of their faces turned toward each other's as he cups the side of her face.

I can't make out any words that he's saying, but I hate the way she's smiling at him right now. I can't fucking take the sight of it and in this moment, I know there is no way I would ever be okay with seeing her with another guy. I want nothing more than to wrap my hands around his throat and stop him from breathing.

Neither of them seem to notice me as I walk in on their little intimate moment, even though my footsteps aren't quiet in the snow. I step around to the front of the bench swing, my hands reaching for

Silas as I curl my fists around the collar of his coat and pull him off.

He doesn't get his feet under him in time, falling to his knees as I drag him away from her. The bench swing shifts and Isla yells out in surprise. I don't bother looking at her, keeping my eyes trained on Silas as he widens his and glares up at me.

"Get your fucking hands off me!" he bellows, reaching for my arms with his hands. At some point while I'm dragging him, he gets his feet back underneath him and rises, standing eye to eye with me. "What the fuck is your problem?"

"I told you before and I won't tell you again," I growl at him, my voice low and cold as I wrap his coat around my fists and tighten it around his throat. "You don't fucking touch her."

Silas chokes out a laugh, his eyes wild and sinister. "You're fucking delusional, man. If she wanted to be with you, do you really think she would have been out here with me?"

My mind barely registers Isla's hands as she pounds on my back with her fists. "Let go of him, Logan!"

"Isla, stay out of this," I bark at her, not letting go of Silas. "He obviously didn't hear me last time, so I'm going to make sure he doesn't forget again. Or else it will be much worse than this."

"Logan," Isla pleads, her voice cracking, and it instantly stops me in my tracks, dragging me out of the pits of my rage. "Please, don't do this. This isn't his fault, it's mine. I was the one who suggested coming outside. It was my idea."

I instantly drop my hands away from Silas and he rubs his throat, leaning forward as he struggles to catch his breath and feed his body the oxygen I was depriving it of. Spinning on my heel, I turn to face Isla, my eyes desperately searching hers for the lie.

"What do you mean it was your idea?"

Her bottom lip quivers and her eyes glisten under the moonlight as the tears begin to fall, staining her cheeks. "I just wanted to forget about you. I told him I wanted to go outside, so he brought me out here." She pauses, hastily swiping the tears from her face as she stares back at me. "After last night, I just wanted something—someone—to help me forget, even if it was only for a few minutes."

My hands find the sides of her face as I step closer to her, my toes touching hers. She tilts her head back, her eyes bouncing back and forth between mine as I get lost in the deep brown hues of her irises. "You don't have to forget, baby. You can try all you want to distract yourself, but you're never going to be able to get rid of me."

"This is fucking ridiculous," Silas grumbles from behind Isla. "Are you really going to put up with this shit? Because you need to choose, Isla. I'm done playing games and done having this asshole intervene every time I get my chance. Who's it going to be? Me or him?"

Isla's glossy eyes don't leave mine. "I'm sorry, Silas."

My heart swells in my chest. Seeing her out here with him threw me into a rage I wasn't sure I would be able to fully come out of. But hearing her admission, the words from her lips, knowing she's mine. It's enough to extinguish the flames that were consuming me from the downward spiral I was heading toward.

I hear Silas say something under his breath as he disappears, but none of it matters. Not with her right here in front of me. My face drops to hers, my mouth crashing into hers as she inhales sharply. Isla relaxes against me, her hands fisting my jacket around my waist as she clings to me. I drain the air from her lungs, my lips moving against hers, our tongues caught in a delicate dance.

She tastes like vodka and orange juice.

And I'm ready to lose myself in this girl.

I break apart from her, both of us coming up for air as I rest my forehead against hers. "It's time to come clean," I whisper, my eyes finding hers under the moonlight. "We need to tell August."

In an instant, the rug is pulled from under our feet. The earth opens up and the ground crumbles away as I hear his voice coming from the darkness of the night.

"You need to tell me what?"

CHAPTER TWENTY-THREE
ISLA

The warmth of Logan's body disappears as we abruptly break apart and step away from each other. Dread fills the pit of my stomach as my heart crawls into my throat. Logan runs a hand through his tousled hair as we both look over to my brother. A shadow passes over August's expression, his eyes angry as he glares at the two of us.

"Would someone like to tell me what the fuck is going on here?"

Nervously shifting the weight on my feet, I wring my hands in front of me. Logan doesn't look at me as he stares down my brother. "It's not what you think."

"Right," August sneers, taking two steps closer

to us. "Because I would be out of my mind to think that my best friend is trying to take advantage of my little sister while she's drunk. That wouldn't make any sense, would it?"

"August." Logan's voice is low, his tone cold, warning. "I promise you that I'm not taking advantage of her. I know how this might look to you right now, but I promise whatever you're thinking is so far off."

Shit.

This was not supposed to happen, he wasn't supposed to find out like this.

"If this isn't you taking advantage of her, then what is it?" August questions him, his feet moving him until he's stopping directly in front of Logan. "Tell me you haven't been fucking around with her behind my back..."

Logan doesn't say anything, a defeated sigh slipping from his lips as he runs his hand down the front of his face. August looks past Logan, his eyes meeting mine as a wave of pain washes over them.

"Isla. Tell me it isn't true..."

I swallow hard over the lump lodged in my throat as I stare into the look of betrayal in my brother's eyes. "I can't do that, August."

His jaw clenches as his eyebrows draw closer

together. "What the fuck," he mutters, looking back at Logan. His eyes focus in on Logan's gaze, his voice loud and cold. "What. The. Fuck."

That's all it takes for my brother to come apart at the seams and completely go off the rails. Logan doesn't anticipate August's movements as he curls his hand into a fist and drives it into Logan's face. He takes the blow, his head jerking to the side as he stumbles backward a few steps.

I've seen Logan fight before and I know what he's capable of. So, when he doesn't react to my brother's attack, my heart breaks for both of them. He stands up straight and instead of bothering to block his face, he stands there and takes it as August throws another fist into his head.

I'm frozen in place, rendered completely immobile. I know I need to step in, to make this stop, but how? Tensions are high and emotions are running wild. The last thing I want to see is them fighting, especially over something to do with me. Something that could have been prevented.

Logan feels like the villain, like he is completely in the wrong and this is what he deserves. He takes everything August gives him, the blows raining down on his face and the sides of his ribs before he loses his balance and falls onto the ground. Logan grunts as August follows him, mumbling obscenities as he straddles Logan's waist and wraps his hands around his throat.

"I told you that I would fucking kill you," he grits out through clenched teeth. "You're my best fucking friend—like my goddamn brother. I trusted you and this is really what you do?"

"August, stop," I yell at him, my mind finally kicking in gear as I rush over. My hands find his shoulders and I'm trying to pull him off Logan, but he doesn't budge. "Don't do this! Please, I'm begging you. You're going to seriously hurt him."

August glances over his shoulder at me, his eyes wild. "Stay out of this, Isla. This is between Logan and I."

"No, it isn't," I plead, my voice cracking as I roughly pull on his shoulders. "This is all my fault."

Logan shakes his head with August's hands still around his throat. "No, it's not," he mouths, his voice barely audible.

My heart shatters into a million pieces, watching his submission as he takes the blame. He's not the only one at fault here. I knew exactly what I was doing. I could have been the one to tell my brother, but instead I chose to stay quiet too. I can't let Logan be the one to take the fall for this.

"August." My grip tightens on his shoulders as my voice grows harder. "Get the fuck off him."

Releasing his shoulders, I take a step back as I inhale deeply and dive into him. He's too big for me to pull off, but at least I can catch him off guard and get him off Logan. My attack throws him off balance and he falls away from Logan, falling onto the ground beside him as I land on top of him.

"What the hell, Isla?" he yells at me as he attempts to shove me away from him. "He fucked up. I warned him and he betrayed me, so it's only right that he pays."

"This isn't Logan's fault. I'm the one who initiated all of this." My eyes desperately search his, looking for the softer side of my brother. The one who can be caring and understanding instead of cold and closed off. "I love him, August."

August freezes, his hands gripping my shoulders as his face falls. "You don't love him, Isla. You *can't*."

I follow August's harsh gaze to Logan, who's sitting on the ground a few feet away from us, watching us carefully. "You don't get to tell me who I can and can't love," I tell my brother, directing my eyes back to his. "I've loved him since we were kids."

"Jesus Christ." His face contorts in something resembling disgust and pain. "How could I be so blind? I knew you had a crush on him, but I didn't think it would ever come to this." August pauses, glancing back at Logan. "Why her, man? You could have chosen anyone, but instead you choose my fucking sister."

Logan's throat bobs as he swallows hard. His lips parting slightly as he lets out a ragged breath. "It wasn't a choice for me—it was never a choice." He pauses, his eyes finding mine through the darkness. "It was written in the stars, August. It was completely inevitable."

"Don't come at me with some fate bullshit," August growls as his hands leave my shoulders and he climbs to his feet. "The two of you were never destined to be together. The only thing you're destined for is ruining each other. And ruining our friendship."

My shoulders sag in defeat, my breath catching in my throat as tears burn the corners of my eyes. "It doesn't have to be like this. We never wanted to hurt you."

August unleashes a harsh laugh as he shakes his head at me. "Too late, sis. You should have just told me from the start."

Logan climbs onto his knees, his lips parting as he watches my brother walk away from the two of us. Tears rapidly fall down my cheeks, smearing my makeup along the way. August's reaction is the exact reason why we were both afraid to tell him, but maybe he was right. Maybe we should have just told him from the start.

"It will be okay, baby," Logan murmurs as he crawls over to me and wraps his arms around me. He pulls me against him, my head falling into his firm chest as I cry against his coat. "I'll talk to him and get him to understand."

Lifting my head, I meet Logan's gaze, my eyes trailing over his bruised and bloodied face. "What if he doesn't?"

Logan swallows hard. "Let me worry about it, okay? This is my problem now, not yours."

"Can we go home?" I ask him, my voice cracking around my words as I stare into his clear blue eyes. "I don't want to be here anymore, and your face is still bleeding."

His lips curl upward as he climbs to his feet and offers his hand for me to take. I slide my palm against his, our fingers lacing together as he lifts me onto my feet. He slides his arm around my back, grabbing my waist as we head around the side of the house, ignoring the party raging inside.

"Let's go home, baby."

CHAPTER TWENTY-FOUR
LOGAN

Since I rode with August to the party, we take an Uber back to the apartment. When we get there, it's dark and quiet inside, with no trace of August. I follow Isla into his bedroom and there is no August there either. Instead, there are clothes thrown around, his drawers hanging wide open, like he packed a bag and left in haste.

He must have come straight here after he left us at the party and since we had to wait for our Uber to show up, we missed him. We were later than him getting back here and he had already packed enough shit for a few days before he left. I know August, he couldn't have gone far. Especially not with having hockey practice and games coming up.

Isla walks out of his room, her shoulders sagging

and head hanging in defeat as I pull out my phone. I don't bother calling Cam, instead I open up my text messages and send him one, hoping August is with him.

> LOGAN
>
> Yo. Have you talked to August at all?

As I walk out of August's bedroom, Isla meets me in the hallway with a first aid kit and grabs my hand before silently pulling me into the kitchen. My phone vibrates in my hand as Isla opens up the kit and takes out the supplies to patch my face.

> CAM
>
> Yeah, he's here. I don't recommend coming here, if that's what you were thinking. Pretty sure he might actually kill you if he sees you.

With the way Cam is able to respond, he must have took a quick nap and slept off some of the alcohol before August showed up there. I can't imagine what he told him, but knowing August, he probably told Cam the truth. Or at least, what he thinks is the truth. He didn't exactly give us any time to fully explain. We had to give him the cliff notes and he wasn't having it.

> LOGAN
>
> I need to talk to him. Can you ask him if we can talk?

I set my phone down on the counter as Isla turns back toward me. "We need to clean some of those cuts on your face." She pauses, her eyes bouncing back and forth between mine. "I can't do anything for the bruises, but we can put some ice on them."

Taking a step backward, I lean against the counter as Isla grabs a gauze pad and some hydrogen peroxide. She pours it onto the pad and presses it against the cut on my forehead before working her way to the one under my eye. I inhale sharply from the sting and watch her face as she focuses on what she's doing.

My phone vibrates on the counter and I grab it, quickly opening a new message from Cam.

> CAM
>
> He said he doesn't want to talk to you tonight. Just let it go, dude, and let him calm down. Call me tomorrow and I'll see if he wants to talk to you then.

I close my phone, locking the screen before I set it back down. "Your brother went to stay at Cam's house." I pause for a moment, wincing as she runs her fingers over the bruise forming under my eye. "He doesn't want to talk right now, but I'm going to try again tomorrow."

Isla stops for a moment, grabbing some antibiotic ointment from the first aid kit. "Maybe I should talk to him instead. Maybe he'll listen to me."

I shake my head as she lifts her hand to apply the ointment to the cuts that August left. "Let me handle it, baby." Her eyes scan my face before finding mine. I know how ridiculous I probably look right now, with healing bruises from the last fight I was in. "This is my mess to clean up."

"No, it's not," she says quietly as she cups the side of my face. "We made this mess together. This isn't just on you to fix now."

I stare back at her, feeling her warm hand against my face as my eyes fall shut. I don't respond, letting her think what she wants instead. We may have made this mess together, but it isn't for her to deal with. She isn't the one who went behind her best friend's back. I'm the one who fucked up, Isla will always be innocent when it really comes down to it.

She wraps her arms around the back of my neck, pulling me against her as she buries her face in my chest. "I'm really sorry, Logan. I never wanted this to happen."

Grabbing her arms, I pull her back slightly, her gaze finding mine as my hands drop to her waist. "It's not your fault, so I don't want you to apologize anymore. Neither of us wanted this to happen, but this is the situation we're in now."

She nods as she draws her bottom lip between her teeth and bites down. I can't take the look on her face right now, as if she doesn't know what to do. To be honest, I'm not quite sure what either of us can do, but with the way that she's looking at me right now, I'm not going to waste this moment... especially when it might be our last.

My grip tightens around her waist and I lift her onto the counter, setting her down as I settle in between her legs. Her arms are still wrapped around the back of my neck and as my lips collide with hers, she slides her fingers along my scalp, gripping locks of my hair.

I breathe her in, drawing the air from her lungs as I swipe my tongue along the seam of her mouth. Isla parts her lips, letting me in as my tongue slides over hers, tangling together. She moves against me, her breathing shallow as she tightens her grip on my hair.

My head screams in protest, but she soothes my wounds with her tongue. I grip the back of her neck, holding her in place as our lips melt together and my other hand slides along her thigh. As I move up her body and slide my hands along the waistband of her pants, she breaks away.

She's breathless, her lust-filled eyes searching mine. "I need you," she breathes, sliding her hands from my hair as she moves them down my back. "Please, Logan."

My eyes search hers as she grabs the bottom hem of my shirt and slides it up my body. We've already fucked up and dug ourselves into a hole that we'll never be able to get out of. The damage has already been done and we officially have everything to lose.

"One last time..."

CHAPTER TWENTY-FIVE
ISLA

Logan lets me pull his shirt over his head and I toss it onto the floor by his feet as he settles back between my legs, his lips instantly colliding with mine. My lips part, letting him in as his tongue slides along mine, tangling together. Instinctively, I wrap my legs around his waist. His palms are warm along my skin as he slides his hands down to my ass and lifts me from the counter.

He carries me through the kitchen, our mouths melting together, but we don't make it any farther than the dining room. He stops by the table, lowering me down onto it as he lets go of me and swipes the table clean from the flower arrangement in the middle. It slides onto the floor, glass shattering and echoing through the apartment as it breaks into shards.

"Fuck it," he murmurs against my lips. "We'll worry about that later. Right now, all I care about is being inside you."

Grabbing the bottom hem of my shirt, I lift it over my head and toss it behind him as he slips his hands around my back, reaching for the clasp of my bra. His eyes are on mine as he releases it and pulls it from my arms. The warmth of his palms warms my soul as he moves his hands to my breasts, cupping them. He drops his face down, drawing one of my nipples into his mouth with his lips. His tongue swirls around the hardened bud, as he rolls the other between his fingertips.

A moan slips from my lips as my head falls back in ecstasy. He sucks on my nipple, lightly nipping at it with his teeth before releasing it. He switches positions, his other hand playing with my nipple that's wet from his saliva as he moves his mouth to the other one. Repeating the same action, he tastes and teases me with his lips and tongue.

I run my hand through his hair, gripping a fistful of it as I moan and pull his head away. "Enough," I murmur, pulling his face back up to mine. "Fuck the foreplay. I want to feel all of you."

Logan's mouth curves and he shakes his head, dropping to his knees between my legs. "I wanna taste this sweet pussy before I'm balls deep inside it." He runs his hands down my torso, the tips of his fingers sliding under the waistband of my pants. "Lie back, baby girl. Let me take care of you."

Swallowing hard, I lower myself down onto the table, lifting my hips as he slides my pants and panties down my thighs, before letting them fall onto the floor by his knees. He places his palms along the inside of my legs, spreading them wide open as his mouth finds my center. His tongue sweeps along my pussy, circling around my clit before he sucks it into his mouth.

My hips instantly buck, a moan slipping from my lips as he works his mouth against me, licking and tasting every inch of my pussy. He knows exactly what he's doing, driving me closer to the brink of ecstasy as he focuses on my clit, rolling his tongue across it over and over again.

"Oh my fucking god," I moan, my hands fisting his head in between my legs.

He lifts his head for a moment, a smirk on his face as his hooded gaze meets mine. "That's right, baby girl. I'm your fucking god."

Logan doesn't give me a chance to respond as he

attacks my pussy again with his mouth. He fucks me with his tongue and I can't take it anymore. I'm so close to the edge and with the way he's working my clit, it doesn't take long until I'm coming apart at the seams, completely losing myself in the abyss of ecstasy.

A warmth spreads through my abdomen, the adrenaline and euphoria quickly riding my system as my orgasm tears through my body. My thighs clamp around his head, but he pins them down with his hands as he continues to feast upon me, tasting every last drop of my orgasm on his tongue. My legs shake as an earthquake rocks my fucking world.

Logan rises to his feet, his face glistening from being between my legs. He wipes it away with the back of his hand. I slowly sit up, my head swimming in the clouds as I ride the lasting waves of my orgasm. Reaching for his pants, I hook my fingers under the waistband of his sweats and begin to push them, along with his boxers, down his thighs.

"How you feeling, baby?" he murmurs as he pushes his pants down to the floor and settles back between my legs again. The tip of his cock presses against my wet pussy and I reach out, attempting to push him away for a moment. His eyes meet mine, his eyebrows drawn together.

"I feel fucking amazing," I breathe, reaching for his throbbing cock with my hand. "But I want to return the favor first."

A fire burns in his eyes as he takes a step back and I slide off the table, dropping to my knees in front of him. His hooded gaze is on mine as I wrap my hand around his length and draw the tip of his cock between my lips. A groan rumbles in his chest, escaping his lips as his head tips back.

"Goddamn, baby girl," he murmurs, his hand stroking my hair as I slide my lips along the length of his cock, drawing him deeper into my mouth. "You're so fucking good."

His words of praise make my pussy tingle, the warmth spreading between my legs and in the pit of my stomach. Moving my hand in tandem with my mouth, my head bobs back and forth, sucking him off as I simultaneously stroke the length of his cock. Logan's hand grips the back of my head, his fingers tangling in my hair.

I continue for a few moments, his breathing growing ragged with every stroke, before he grips my hair harder and stops me as his cock leaves my mouth. "I need to be inside you. Now."

A smile plays on my lips as he hauls me to my feet. He grips my hips, spinning me around to face the table. His palm is hot on my skin as he slides it along my spine, pushing me down against the dining room table as he reaches the base of my neck.

"I'm gonna fuck you from behind, baby." He pauses for a moment, dragging his tongue along my spine as he leans over me. His lips brush against my ear. "You wanna feel my balls slapping against your pussy as I fuck you senseless?"

The warmth in the pit of my stomach grows, spreading through my body, and my pussy is dripping as he runs his tongue along the outer shell of my ear. "God, yes. Fuck me, Logan. Fuck me until I forget."

The tip of his cock presses against me and he moves away from my back, lifting my hips higher until my feet are off the ground. In one swift movement, he slides inside me, filling me completely as he plunges deep inside. I feel him in my fucking ribs, moaning out in pain and pleasure from the thickness of his length.

"Mmmm, let me hear you, baby girl."

His fingertips bite into my flesh as he tightens his grip on my hips, slowly sliding his cock out before pounding back into me again. His balls slap into me, another sensation erupting through my body as they move against my clit.

"Don't stop," I breathe, turning my head to the side as I rest it on the dining room table.

Logan slides his palm along my spine, stopping as he reaches the base of my neck. He grips the back of my neck with one hand as the other grasps my hip, and he begins to move his hips. Every thrust is harder than the one before, his hips rocking into me as his cock fills me to the brim.

The sounds of our moans and skin on skin fill the apartment. His balls slap against my pussy, hitting my clit with every thrust. He picks up the pace, pounding into me as he does exactly what he promised, and fucks me senseless.

I'm a fucking mess, climbing closer and closer to the edge. He slams into me once more, sending me falling over the cliff. I cry out in ecstasy, my orgasm rocking my body as he follows directly behind me. Together we fall, into the depths of our euphoric abyss. I'm lost in him; he's lost in me.

And I never want either of us to be found.

CHAPTER TWENTY-SIX
LOGAN

Rolling over in bed, I see Isla sleeping next to me and a smile touches my lips. Her face is relaxed and so innocent as she softly snores. After fucking her on the dining room table, we moved into her bed for the night and didn't fall asleep until early morning. I don't want to disturb her and wake her up, but I fucking hate leaving her right now. I need to go make everything better and fix things, but I'm afraid this might be the last time I get to see her like this.

She's become my world—the most important thing. And dare I say, she's more important to me than the game I've devoted my life to. My best friend, her brother, is still important, but it's a different type of relationship. There was a point where I wasn't sure I wanted to jeopardize that.

But now it's already been ruined, I don't know what to do.

I don't want to have to choose between the two of them. If I were to choose Isla, August would never forgive me and he would never approve. If I chose him instead of her, how the hell would she ever forgive me for that? She wouldn't. Regardless of what happens when I go see August today, someone is going to get hurt.

Leaning toward Isla, I gently press my lips to her temple before pulling away. She moans softly, stirring in her sleep, but she doesn't wake up. Grabbing the comforter, I pull the covers over her, tucking them in beneath her chin as I climb out of the bed.

It was wrong of me to go and sleep with her again, especially after August finding out what had been going on, but I don't really care at this point. I needed to feel her against me one last time, just in case it were to be the last time. I needed the opportunity to fully savor her before I would never have a taste again.

I quickly get dressed and quietly slip out of the room without her waking up. Even though Cam told me to call, I ignore his instructions and send him a text message letting him know I'm on my way. It would be more respectful of me to let August tell me when he's ready to talk, but fuck that.

This needs to be taken care of now. I'm not waiting around for him to give me his permission. We need to talk and hash this out before it gets worse. Before I get in deeper with his sister… although, I'm not sure that's even possible at this point. She's already worked her way under my skin and embedded herself in my soul. She crawled into my rib cage and made a home in my heart. There's no way to get her out of there now.

When I get to Cam's, he's already waiting for me, sitting outside on his front stoop as he smokes a cigarette. He keeps it hidden from most people, especially our coach because that is something that would never fly with him being on the team. But when he's really stressed out, it's what he turns to, to calm down.

"How is he?" I ask Cam as I walk up to the stoop and lean against the railing.

He lifts his eyes, pulling his sunglasses farther down his nose as he assesses me. "Shit. He looks a hell of a lot better than you do. Did you not defend yourself at all?"

I shrug. "Why would I? I deserved everything he gave me."

Cam shakes his head as he exhales a cloud of smoke. "Seriously. I can't believe you slept with his sister, although I can't say I'm fully surprised."

"What's that supposed to mean?" I ask him, watching as he puts out his cigarette and flicks it into the trash can a few feet away.

"Dude, do you forget that we've known each other forever?" He purses his lips as he stares at me. "I've seen the way the two of you looked at each other. I just didn't think you would actually have the balls to go for her."

Cam stands up and I follow him to the front door. As he pulls it open, August is already standing on the other side, as if he was just about to walk outside. He's been expecting me, whether he wants to see me or not. And judging by the way he glares at me, I think it's safe to say he isn't thrilled to be seeing me right now.

I don't miss the look of satisfaction that passes through his eyes as he sees the damage he left on my face. "Outside," he growls at me, motioning with his head for me to stay on the front stoop. Cam brushes past him, staying silent as he walks into the house while August walks out.

I walk down the steps, stopping on the sidewalk as I turn around to face him. August moves away from the door, dropping down onto the top step as he tilts his head to the side and narrows his eyes at me.

"You wanted to talk, so fucking talk."

Swallowing hard over the lump lodged in my throat, I nod. "I've been in love with her for a long time, August. I don't expect you to understand, but none of this is random and it's not personal. It started in high school, but we never did anything then."

"Oh, how fucking noble of you," he sneers, rolling his eyes. "That's mighty big of you to wait until my sister turned eighteen before fucking her."

"It's not like that, man," I tell him, the desperation evident in my voice. Pausing, I run a frustrated hand through my hair. "I want more with her, but I won't do that without your blessing. You're both important to me, but if you don't want me with her, I can't argue with you on that. I know I'm not the perfect person. Hell, you of all people know of all of my shortcomings. I can't say I would blame you if you didn't want me to date her. I've always told her that she deserves more than I could ever give her, but she never accepted that as an answer."

August keeps his narrowed eyes on me. "She does deserve more. I know how you operate. When it comes down to it, the game will always be more important to you. Hockey is your first love—your life—just like your fucking dad's. And when it falls to shit, I refuse to sit back and watch you destroy her life like your father did to your mother."

Whoa.

His words hit me like a ton of bricks straight to the chest. The force hits me harder than his fists ever could and I'm left with nothing, staring at him as my eyes widen. It was a low blow and he knows it, the guilt instantly washing over his face.

My father was never a part of my life, but I was told the story from my mother. When she was pregnant with me, there were complications and she couldn't move to the state where he got drafted on a team. One night when he was coming home to see her, he got in a car accident that ruined his career. He was never the same again and he left when I was only six months old, without ever reaching out again, until recently.

I don't personally know the man and never really cared to, even after he reached out to my mom after all this time. But hearing this from August fucking hurts. He knows my father was never involved in my life, so how could he expect me to really be like him? Although, if there's one thing I've been trying to do in my life, it's to make sure that I wouldn't end up like him.

August isn't wrong. Hockey is my first love, the first thing that I fully dedicated myself to. It has always been my life, but I'm learning that there is more to life than just playing the game. When I really think about it after he said it, would I choose Isla over the sport? If something happened and I was in the same situation as my father, would I end up the same way he did?

He's wrong in that fact. I would never leave my wife and kid just because my career was ruined. It's not that important to me, when it really comes down to it. But as August's words swirl around in my mind, I can't help but think that he's right.

"I would never do that to her," I tell him, my voice low and quiet. "I would never fucking leave her and my kid just because of my career being ruined."

"How could you possibly know that?" he demands, the guilt still swirling in his eyes, but there's no way to backtrack now. "You can't guarantee shit, Logan. You fucking told me I had nothing to worry about when I had suspicions of you two.

You need to end shit with her now. Let her find someone else, someone who she can be happy with."

I stare back at him, his eyes burning holes through mine. I don't want to agree with him, but he's never going to let me live this down. He's never going to forgive me for this and if I try to further pursue things with Isla, it's only going to make the situation worse. It destroyed our friendship and I don't want to come between the two of them and their relationship.

"Okay. You want me to walk away from her, fine," I tell him, the words bitter on my tongue as I spit them out. I instantly regret it because it's not what I want, but he's backed me into a corner. I have no choice but to submit. "You think she'll be happier without me, then I will let her go."

"Good," he says, glancing at the ground as he moves his feet in his slides. "I just want her to have the chance to see there's more to life out there. Her entire life has been hockey because of me. She doesn't need to keep living this fucking life, bro. I just want her to be happy, but I can't support it being with my best friend."

I don't fully understand his reasoning, but I nod anyway. He either spoke the truth about me ending up like my father or it was solely out of him being hurt. Either way, I'm not going to explore it. Not when it feels like my heart was just ripped out of my chest.

Not when I know that I need to go home and rip Isla's from her rib cage.

"She'll be fine," August tells me, his voice soft and quiet. His eyes meet mine and he frowns. "It was just a crush that got out of hand. She'll get over it and see I was right. And you'll do the same, like you always do. You'll move from one bed to the next."

"Is that why you really don't want her with me?"

August cuts his eyes at me. "I fucking know you, Logan Knight. You're a good guy, don't get me wrong. You're my best fucking friend for a reason. But the two of you don't belong together. You'll hurt her in the end and then I'll really have to kill you, and I'm afraid I won't be able to do it."

I stare back at him, his words fully sinking in. Maybe our friendship isn't fully over and maybe it wouldn't be if I dated his sister, but he's afraid of when it would end. And because there's no guarantee, he doesn't trust that we wouldn't break up—that this is a forever love. He's afraid that I'll hurt her and then our friendship would really be over.

"How do we get back to where we were?" I ask him, dropping down onto the bottom step as I stare at the cracks in the concrete sidewalk. "I know I betrayed you and broke your trust."

"Yeah, you fucking did," he breathes, a sigh falling from his lips as he rises to his feet. "End things with my sister and that's a start."

I hear him moving behind me, but as I turn around to look at him, he disappears back into Cam's house without another word. He leaves me alone in the silence, with nothing but my thoughts and his parting words hanging heavily in the air.

I have no choice but to end things with Isla.

And she's never going to forgive me.

CHAPTER TWENTY-SEVEN
ISLA

Sitting on the couch, I twirl a stray string from the blanket between my fingers. Logan was gone when I woke up this morning and I wasn't surprised to find the apartment empty. He mentioned last night that he needed to patch things up with my brother, however that might look or end up.

I didn't call him or text him after I woke up because I knew he was going to be at Cam's. And if he was with my brother, me reaching out to him wouldn't look good. If anything, it would only make our situation worse. I'm just afraid for him to come home... I'm afraid to hear what August had to say.

I absentmindedly flip through the channels when I hear the front door open. My body falls rigid before I sit up straighter, turning to face the dining room as my breath catches in my throat. I listen as the door shuts, and his footsteps are heavy as he walks through the kitchen.

Logan pauses, his face falling as he stops in the dining room. His ocean blue eyes find mine and there's a storm brewing within the depths. His plump lips are situated in a frown, his eyebrows drawn together as he walks toward me.

He doesn't say a word as he walks around the couch, dropping down onto the cushion beside me. His hands find my arms as he pulls me toward him, burying his face in my neck as he wraps himself around me. There's something off about him, the way he's acting, but I breathe him in, savoring the smell of his cologne and the warmth of his body.

"This has to stop, baby," he murmurs, his lips brushing against the sensitive skin on my neck. "We can't keep doing this anymore."

My heart pounds erratically in my chest as I freeze against him. "What are you talking about?" My voice is quiet, my words broken as the panic seeps into the cracks. "We can't keep doing what?"

"This," he says softly as he presses his lips to the column of my throat and pulls away. "We can't be together. We can't do this together. I have to let you go, let you move on and find someone that can give you everything you deserve."

My heart sinks and the floor falls from beneath me as dread fills the pit of my stomach. This can't be happening. After everything we've been through together, this is where we really ended up. With both of our hearts broken, in shattered shards scattered across the floor.

"I don't need to find someone because I already have," I tell him, my voice cracking as the tears fall from my eyes without warning. A lump forms in my throat and I swallow roughly over it. "That person is you."

His bright blue eyes search mine, his hands stroking the sides of my face, catching the tears with the pads of his thumbs as they fall. "I know, baby, but your brother doesn't approve and that's not fair to you. The last thing I want to do is come between the two of you, so I have to let you go."

"No," I shake my head, the overwhelming panic consuming me. It's like we're repeating the past and I'm living through him leaving me again. It's different this time, though. There's more feelings involved and we're in so goddamn deep. It's more than just a crush. I love him. "Let me talk to him and get him to understand. It doesn't have to be this way, Logan. You don't have to choose. Just let me talk to him first."

Logan's smile is sad. "I'm sorry, baby. It does have to be this way. He wouldn't listen to me and he's not going to want to hear it from you either." He pauses, taking both sides of my face in his hands as his wet eyes probe mine. "We just need to take this little break and let August breathe. Maybe he'll change his mind. And if he doesn't, you still have a chance to find happiness instead of being stuck with your high school crush."

"You're more than that, Logan," I breathe, my voice barely audible as my eyebrows draw together. "I meant what I said. I love you—I've loved you for a long time."

"I love you too, Isla." He smiles, his eyes close as two tears slip out and fall down the sides of his face. "That's why I have to let you go."

His lips find mine, his kiss slow and brutal. He kisses me like it's the last time he ever will, and there's a good chance it might be. If August never comes around to the thought of the two of us together, Logan will never come back to me.

He slowly pulls away from me, his soft lips touching my forehead before he rises to his feet. I watch him as he walks away from the couch, heading back toward the dining room. It's an awkward position, given that we both live in the same apartment.

"Don't fucking do this, Logan Knight," I choke out, my voice hard and cold as I glare at him.

Logan glances at me over his shoulder as he pauses in the doorway that leads into the kitchen. "I'm sorry," his voice is barely audible and his eyes are filled with pain as the distance between us feels like it grows by the second. "I'll always love you, Isla Whitley."

And with that, he disappears from the dining room. His footsteps are heavy as he walks through the kitchen and the tears don't stop falling from my face. A sob tears through me as I hear the door shut behind him, and I'm left alone with my thoughts and my heart ripped to shreds and discarded on the floor.

I can't believe he really did this to me—to us.

I shouldn't be surprised, though…

I always knew he would be the one to hurt me.

CHAPTER TWENTY-EIGHT
LOGAN

It feels strange. This morning, I was breaking Isla's heart and now I'm stepping onto the ice for a game, like my life isn't currently in shambles. August skates past me, not saying a word as I adjust my gloves on my hands. I wouldn't expect him to give me the time of day right now, but we both have to play and perform like everything around us doesn't matter.

Despite our differences and me completely fucking him over, we have to play nicely together because our teammates are depending on us. Even though I'm sure he wants to beat my face in, we can't hash it out again. Plus, I did exactly what he asked of me. Not only for him, but for her too.

I just hope I made the right decision.

I stretch my legs, skating as my body warms up, and the ice makes my legs cold. I can't actually feel it, though. Nothing really seems to matter, not with this empty feeling in my chest. My heart left a hole in my rib cage when Isla took it with her. Usually, skating was the one thing that could distract me, to bring some sense of happiness back into my life, but even now, it just doesn't quite reach the hollowness inside.

We skate around for a few more minutes before lining up in our positions for the puck drop. August leans down in front of the other center, his stick ready to meet the puck during the face-off. Tensions between us are still high and that's going to be August's driving force right now. He's going to play like he's never played before because he can't take it out on me.

I glance up at the stands as I wait for the ref to come over to them. My eyes scan the seats and when I find the ones reserved for family, I notice my mom is sitting there, but Isla is nowhere to be seen. My heart sinks. I shouldn't have expected her to be here, but it would have been nice to see her again.

Especially because now I'm going to have to move out of that fucking apartment. There's no way I can live with her and August after everything that has happened. And I'm not going to have either of them be displaced. If anything, I'm the one to go. Thankfully, my mom moved to the city when I left for school, so when I talked to her this morning, she said I could come stay at her and my stepfather Owen's house.

I'm too distracted when the puck drops and August wins the face-off. I don't notice until the puck slides across the ice, completely missing the blade of my stick as I stare absentmindedly at the empty seats.

"What the fuck, Knight?" Sterling barks at me as he skates past me. "Get your head out of your ass."

I swallow hard, the frustration burning in my veins as I nod at him before pushing off on my skates. Thankfully, Cam grabbed the puck before the other team did and turned it around, skating toward their goal as he passes it to August in the center of the arena. Shaking my head at myself, I push away the thoughts of Isla and focus on the task at hand.

This might not be an important game, but if you treat every one like it's similar to a playoff game, it helps keep your head in it and out of the clouds. There comes a time where you have to leave everything else off the ice and the only thing that matters is the stick in your hand and the puck sliding across the ice.

Putting my head down, I skate toward the blue line, hanging back as I watch our offense pass the puck back and forth before the right wing from the other team slaps it away from them. It comes soaring down my way and I skate after it, sliding my stick along it as I take the puck around the back of the net. Asher, our goalie, nods at me and the ref blows the whistle for an icing.

Stickhandling the puck, my skates effortlessly slide over the ice as I look for someone to pass it to. The other team's offense is right in my face and I see August hanging by the center. I slice the puck, sending it over to him as he spins around with it, slipping past the player on him. He's wide open and skates his ass off as he makes a break for it.

He glances around and Cam isn't far behind him, but there's no sense in passing it. Cam is shouting at him to shoot the puck and the other team's goalie drops down into a butterfly stance in an attempt to block August's shot. He swipes his stick, lifting the puck as he sends it directly into the top shelf of the net.

The horn sounds and everyone in the stands starts yelling. August pumps his fist in the air, skating around in a circle as everyone on our team goes up to congratulate him like he had just scored the game-winning goal. That's how it is with a team that's like family. We celebrate every fucking victory.

I'm the last one in the small line and I skate over to August, tapping the top of his helmet with my glove. "Nice shot, man."

He stares at me through his cage and I see the corners of his lips tilt upward in the slightest bit. "Thanks, bro." He nods at me, his eyes different from earlier. Softer. I watch him as he skates back to the center ice and I take my position by the blue line again, waiting for the puck to drop.

The puck drops and August wins the face-off, sending it back to me. I head toward the center of the rink before passing it as someone yells shift change from the bench. August and I skate off the ice together, hopping over the boards as Simon and Greyson take our places on the ice.

Grabbing a bottle of water, I pour some into my mouth through the cage of my helmet as August does the same. We both sit in silence for a moment, staring out at the ice as we watch our teammates fight for the puck.

I look over to say something to him, just as Sterling gets slammed into the boards on the other side of the rink by the opposing team. I rise to my feet, staring out as he drops to the ice before getting back up. "What the fuck! That was a dirty-ass hit and the refs really aren't going to call that shit?!"

"Of course not," August mutters, shaking his head in disgust as he rises to his skates beside me. "That was complete bullshit."

I glance up at the scoreboard, noting there's still nine minutes left in the period and it isn't close to my time to get back on the ice, but my blood boils from the dirty hit. Sterling is skating slower than he was before he got hit. My eyes find the 27 on the back of the jersey who hit him.

"Shift change!" I bellow, slapping my stick against the boards. My ass is already about to hop over them before Greyson skates back over. "Fucking shift change!"

Greyson is barely over the boards as I'm hopping out onto the ice, my eyes locked on Number 27 skating toward their net as Simon barrels toward it. I need to hang back and collect myself. I can't go into this and beat the shit out of him, but he got away with a dirty-ass hit and even though the refs didn't call it, I'm not letting that shit fly.

Their goaltender catches the puck as Simon sends it flying toward him, and the ref blows his whistle. I skate toward the center of the rink as they line up for a face-off closer to the goal. Number 27 isn't far from me and I'm coming for that motherfucker this time.

I watch Sterling skate over and hop onto the bench as Leander gets in the lineup. The puck drops and the other team wins the face-off. Their center skates down the middle and I see Number 27 coming closer to me as I skate closer to the net to defend it. Moving across the ice, I come up beside him, checking him hard into the boards as I steal the puck from him.

"Fuck!" he yells out in anger as I skate away, passing the puck to Simon who is closer to the center ice. He gets my pass and heads back down the rink toward their goal. Number 27 glares at me before skating away. "You're fucking done," he calls over his shoulder.

A smile creeps onto my lips and I skate after them, hanging back a bit as the puck is in the offensive zone. He's got it all wrong. He acts like he's going to do some shit to me, but I'm the one who has unfinished business with him. I wait for them, watching as they fight over the puck. I slowly start to skate backward as they move back toward our net.

Number 27 has the puck and instead of going toward the net, he's barreling straight toward me. I wait until he's literally inches from me before I duck out of the way and he sends himself into the boards. He slams into them with a loud smack, falling to his knees for a moment. A laugh rumbles in my chest and I shake my head at his stupidity.

He's really fucking targeting me, but he managed to knock himself down without me having to touch him.

"Shift change!" someone yells from our bench and I glance over to see who it is. August is standing there, waving me to come back, but I shake my head and glance up at the stands.

I don't know what compels me to do it, but it's almost as if I could feel her eyes on me, even with so much distance between us. My eyes look up to where my mother is and much to my surprise, I find Isla sitting next to her.

A smile creeps onto my lips, even though I know I shouldn't be smiling, but I'm fucking elated seeing her here. The girl who occupies every thought inside my head.

"LOGAN!" August's voice is loud, but I almost don't hear it over how deafening the game is. "LOOK OUT!"

I glance down at him, my eyebrows drawn together before I look to my right, just as Number 27 comes flying toward me. There's not enough time to get out of his way and he completely body slams into me, with such a dirty fucking hit as he violently shoves me into the boards.

I don't anticipate the full force of his hit and my head slams into the glass before I have the chance to brace myself for any of it. Even my helmet isn't enough to stop the instant whiplash that I get. Time feels as if it's suspended as the corners of my vision go black and rapidly closing in on me as I fall in slow motion.

Everything goes dark before I hit the ice.

CHAPTER TWENTY-NINE
ISLA

"LOGAN!" I scream his name, watching as his tall form crumples onto the ice like a rag doll. Camilla is already out of her seat, running down the steps in her heels, and I'm not far behind her. My lungs constrict and my heart pounds rapidly in my chest.

Oh my god, this is all my fault.

Logan was too busy looking at me, distracted when he saw me sitting in the stands he didn't even see that player coming directly toward him. Number 27 was on a mission to fuck Logan up and he accomplished that when he slammed him into the boards with no mercy.

The entire arena falls silent. The other guys on Logan's team surround Number 27, and August is off the bench, throwing his gloves onto the ice as he skates directly toward the guy, ready to fight him. The other team gets involved and it's suddenly a full-out brawl going down on the ice.

I watch in fucking horror as Logan lies on the ice, the paramedics quickly surrounding him. The refs can't get the players under control and some who don't even fight are throwing fists and tossing their helmets off as it escalates and gets violent.

Camilla grabs my hand, dragging me away from the rink as we slip out into the concourse and we head toward the stairs that lead down to the locker rooms. No one bothers to question her as we push past security. They know exactly who she is and not to fuck with her. Especially when that's her son lying on the ice.

My heart is in my throat and my stomach is at my feet. I feel so fucking helpless and so goddamn scared. Camilla pushes down the tunnel toward the ice where they're wheeling out a stretcher. Tears are in my eyes, already falling as they stream down my face. This can't be happening right now.

"What the hell is going on?" Camilla demands, stepping out onto the ice in her heels as they lift him on the stretcher. "Is he responsive?"

One of the paramedics shakes his head. "He's

completely unconscious but he is breathing. We need to get him to the hospital immediately."

I press my back against the wall, giving them space as they wheel him past. One of the paramedics pulled Logan's helmet off and his head is turned in my direction. He looks so peaceful with his eyes closed, except for the bruises and cuts that are changing colors on his face.

My beautifully broken boy...

Camilla follows after them and I walk back toward the ice, just in time as the refs finally have everyone separated. August catches sight of me at the end of the tunnel and quickly skates over.

"Don't worry, the asshole that hit him is kicked out of the game and hopefully the rest." He pauses for a moment, his eyes searching mine as the tears continue to stream down my cheeks.

"Isla, we have to go!" Camilla injects as she calls for me from the opposite end of the tunnel.

August frowns, his eyebrows drawn together as he stares at me with a worried look passing through his eyes. "Go with her," he says softly, motioning for me to turn around. "Go make sure he's okay."

I nod, hiccuping as I hastily wipe the tears away from my face. I quickly move toward him, wrapping my arms around his waist even though he towers over me on his skates. "I love you, big brother."

"I love you too, little sis," he murmurs, hugging me back before he pushes me away. "Now go."

Nodding, I quickly spin on my heel and rush down the tunnel toward Camilla. She's already gone and I break out into a sprint as I see her walking through the concourse and toward the exit. I'm out of breath when I catch up to her. She pushes open the door, holding it open for me as we step out into the cold air.

"They said they were taking him to Samaritan Memorial Hospital. It's only about ten minutes away, but we have to meet him there."

"Okay," I say softly, following her to her car. "Are you sure it's okay if I come along with you."

Camilla pauses as she pulls open the driver's-side door. "Of course, sweetie. You're like family." She drops down into her seat and I do the same in the passenger's seat. "I know how Logan feels about you. He called me this morning and told me everything. If anyone belongs by his side right now, I know in my heart that it's you."

My breath catches in my throat and my heart rattles in its cage as my chest constricts. I can feel the tears burning the corners of my eyes again and

I'm a damn mess all over again. The tears fall down the sides of my face and I glance out the window as I wipe them away.

We're both silent on the ride to the hospital, each of us lost in our own thoughts. I know Camilla went through hell when her ex-husband had his accident and I'm sure this is like living it all over again. This isn't the first time Logan has been hurt during a game, but it's the first time he took a hit like that and had to be taken out on a stretcher.

That's her son—her one and only in life. I can't imagine how she's feeling right now, not knowing if he's okay or what is really going on. The way his head hit the glass... the thought alone makes me cringe as a shiver slides down my spine.

He has to be okay. Everything we have can't end like this.

Our story isn't over yet, even if he tried to end things with me this morning. I didn't want to accept it then, and I sure as hell don't accept it now.

He has to be okay...

When we get to the hospital, Camilla doesn't bother finding a parking spot. Instead, she pulls up directly out at the front of the building and marches inside. I follow after her, wishing I had half the confidence this woman does. I'm envious of the way she carries herself, like no one can touch her or tell her what she can or can't do.

She strides to the front desk of the emergency room, her heels loud on the linoleum floor. I'm right behind her, hovering as she barks out her son's name, demanding to know where he is and what is going on.

The polite woman at the desk tells us that the ambulance just arrived a few minutes ago and he's in the trauma bay right now, so we aren't allowed to go back yet. I swear Camilla is about to riot when she begins to raise her voice, demanding she speaks to someone above her.

The woman cowers and disappears as she gets her supervisor. Her supervisor comes over and Camilla explains the entire situation to her, demanding that she sees Logan or she will speak to someone on the board. Camilla is intimidating as fuck and I love it. The supervisor bends and tells her she can only allow one of us to go back.

Camilla glances at me, her eyes sad, but they're filled with more panic than I've ever seen swimming in someone's gaze. "Isla..." her voice trails off but I know what she's going to say. Logan is her son. If anyone should be with him right now, it's her.

"Go," I tell her, nodding my head toward the

woman who's waiting to take Camilla to Logan. "I'll wait to hear from you for when it's my turn to go see him."

Camilla pulls me in for a quick hug before she shuffles across the waiting room to the receptionist who is waiting for her. I watch them through tears as they disappear through the sliding glass doors that lead into the emergency room.

I find an empty seat along the back wall, away from most of the people waiting, and I drop my head into my hands as the tears completely consume me. A sob racks through my body and the panic sets in. I know I was more in shock when it first happened and now the reality of the situation is setting in.

They have him in the trauma bay, so that can't be good at all. I don't know much about medicine, but I've watched a few doctor drama shows in my years. I don't think that's the place you want to be in the hospital, but if that's the level of care he needs, then he has to be in the right place.

A million things run through my mind. The way he hit his head, does he have some kind of head trauma? Jesus, this is too much. I don't know if I can even take it. Without thinking, I rise to my feet and leave the waiting room, the cold evening air stings my face as I step outside and begin to pace.

I pace back and forth—back and forth. I'm losing track of time. I'm losing my mind without knowing what is going on. My feet don't stop moving until my legs are aching and my heels feel like there are blisters forming.

Headlights flash as another car pulls up in front of the hospital, but I don't bother letting it distract me from the thought of him. That's the only thing my mind can focus on right now. Logan, lying back there on a hospital bed and the millions of what-ifs running through my head.

"Isla," my brother calls out, his footsteps getting louder as he walks over to me. I lift my head from my gaze being on the ground, my eyes widening as I see him, Cam and Sawyer all walking toward me. "The other guys are on their way here too."

A sob catches in my throat, the tears instantly filling my eyes as my heart swells for Logan's family. All of these guys—his teammates—they're his family. And they're coming here to sit in the waiting room until we get some answers.

August's face falls, and his brows draw together as he frowns. "How is he? Do you know what's going on?"

I shake my head, swallowing roughly over the

lump lodged in my throat. "Camilla went back with him after we got here. All I know is that they had him in the trauma bay. I haven't heard anything since then."

"Shit," Cam mutters, walking past me as he brings a cigarette to his lips and lights the end of it. The cherry burns brightly in the night, the smoke mixing with our breaths as he exhales in a rush. "I swear to Christ, if something happens to him, I'm going to paralyze the motherfucker who did this to him."

The scene replays again in my head and a sob breaks out from me before I can swallow it back. August is instantly in front of me, wrapping his arms around me as he pulls me in for a hug.

"He'll be okay, Isla," he murmurs, brushing my hair back with one of his hands. "This is Logan we're talking about. He's one stubborn asshole. You know he'll make it out of this."

Turning my head to the side, I rest my cheek on his firm chest, my tears soaking through his sweatshirt. "But what if he doesn't?"

August doesn't say anything and only hugs me tighter, his hand still stroking my hair like Mom always did when we needed to be comforted. I want to believe my brother, to agree with him and be positive. I want him to be right, but what if he's wrong about this?

I need him to be okay…

Because I'm not so sure I can live in this world without him.

CHAPTER THIRTY
LOGAN

My head throbs and screams in protest as I attempt to peel my eyelids open. They feel so heavy, as if they're weighed down by sandbags. I hear a faint beeping sound in the distance, but I can't quite make out what it is without fully opening my eyes. Even though my body fights against me, I slowly open them.

The lights in the room are dim and it's quiet, except for the beeping from a machine to my right. The throbbing in my head increases as I turn it to the side, finding my mom sitting beside my bed. My hand is in between both of hers and she rests her forehead on the mattress.

"Mom?" I croak, my voice rough and harsh. My

throat burns as I struggle to get the word out, but she hears me.

She lifts her head in a rush, her bloodshot eyes wide as they find mine. "Oh my god, Logan," she breathes, a smile forming on her lips as her eyes fill with tears. "You're awake."

I attempt to lift my head, the confusion hanging heavily in my hazy brain as my eyes try to scan the room. My vision goes blurry for a moment before focusing again, and I drop my head back down in defeat. "What happened?"

Her eyes are soft, her eyebrows drawn together with nothing but sympathy swimming in the blue depths of her eyes. "You don't remember? You had a hockey game last night and got hit pretty hard." She pauses, exhaling a deep breath. "You had a pretty bad concussion and have been out for almost twenty-four hours. The doctors said there was no bleeding or swelling, but your brain got rattled hard enough to have you sleeping that long."

My brain struggles against the memory, but it comes back to me in a rush and I remember it all. Number fucking 27 and that goddamn dirty hit. And Isla. She showed up for the game, and she was sitting in the stands beside my mom when it happened.

My heart crawls into my throat. "Where is Isla?"

"She's right there," my mother smiles, pointing to the other side of the room where Isla is curled up on a couch. "She hasn't left since we got here."

Goddamn. I can't even stop it as tears fill my eyes. My heart swells in my chest and a lump forms in my throat as I stare at her small form sleeping peacefully. She saw the entire accident happen and she's still here. I never would have expected her to stay by my side this entire time, but that's Isla Whitley.

She's a ride or die type of girl.

My girl.

"Do you want me to wake her up?" my mother asks softly, her eyes searching mine.

"No." I smile at her as I wipe the tears from my eyes. "Let her get some rest. I'm sure she's exhausted if she's been here since the game."

My mom's lips curl upward as she flashes her bright white teeth at me. "Actually, your entire team is here." She pauses, squeezing my hand that she's still holding. "They've been camped out in the waiting room since your accident."

"Are you serious?" My voice cracks. Having Isla here means the world to me, but knowing that my entire team is here—my entire family—I don't even have words for it. When bad shit happens, it's funny how it really brings everyone together. How they actually show up for you. Those are the important people in life, the ones you should never let go of.

My mother nods eagerly. "Let me go get the nurse so the doctor can come check on you. August has been asking to come back as soon as you were awake."

"He's been here too?"

"Of course, sweetie," my mom tells me, her voice soft and warm, her eyes sympathetic. "He loves you like a brother. You're his best friend. He's been in and out of this room, waiting for you to wake up too."

I nod, my heart crawling into my throat. "Go get the nurse."

"On my way now." My mother smiles as she rises to her feet and presses her lips to my forehead. "I'm so goddamn happy to hear your voice."

"I love you, mom," I tell her, my eyes growing heavy as she says it back to me before leaving the room. I let my eyelids fall shut and drift back asleep for a few moments until the nurse and the doctor walk in.

They do an exam, carefully checking over me to make sure everything seems okay. The doctor turns to talk to me after hanging her stethoscope back around her neck. "You seem to be doing well and being awake is a good sign. You didn't sustain any significant injuries, but you had a pretty bad concussion. Your brain still needs time to heal, so you're going to have to take some time off from hockey until a neurologist clears you."

"How long will that be?" I can't contain the panic that snakes itself around my words. I've had concussions and injuries in the past, but nothing this significant.

The doctor puts her hands in her pockets as the nurse checks my vital signs one last time and asks my mother if we need anything. "It could be anywhere from two to four weeks, so it isn't that much time. But we're going to set up a follow-up appointment for you with neuro once you're discharged, so they will clear you after your appointment as long as you don't have any symptoms."

"Okay." I nod and wince, glancing to the other side as I see movement from the couch. Isla slowly sits up, throwing the blanket off of her. Her eyes find mine and they widen as she sees I'm awake. A smile forms on my lips and she covers her mouth with her hand. "When will I be discharged?"

"We'll probably keep you one more night, just for observation, and then I don't see why you wouldn't be able to leave tomorrow morning."

Isla rises to her feet, and my mother thanks the doctor before she and the nurse leave the room again. I look back at Isla, my expression soft as my eyes search hers.

"Come here, baby."

My mom turns around, her gaze following mine as she sees Isla walking closer to the bed. She looks back at me, her eyes wet as she smiles brightly at me. "I'll give you guys some time alone," she tells me as she rises to her feet and moves out of the way for Isla who walks directly toward me. "August wants to see you next, so let me know when I should send him in."

"Thanks, Mom," I tell her before directing my attention back to Isla as my mom slips out of the room. Lifting my arms, I reach out for her and she drops down onto the mattress beside me as I wrap my arms around her, enveloping her against my body. She's warm and smells just like vanilla, like my girl.

"I was so worried about you," she breathes, wrapping her arms around me as she rests her head on my shoulder. "When I saw you hit the ice and not get up, that might have been the scariest moment of my life, Logan. Don't you dare scare me like that again."

A chuckle vibrates in my chest and I bury my face in her hair, breathing her in as I press my lips against the top of her head. "I wasn't trying to scare you. I didn't even see him coming because I was too busy focusing on you in the stands."

"Well, maybe I shouldn't come to any more of your games if I'm just going to be a distraction." She pauses for a moment, her palm warm against my skin through the hospital gown I'm still wearing. "You know that when you're on the ice, nothing else matters except for winning that game. If you're going to be too busy watching me in the stands, you're going to get hit like that again and it could be even worse next time."

"Don't be stupid," I laugh, wrapping my arms tighter around her. "I want you at every single one of my games. I promise that after the puck drops, I'll make sure to pay attention to what I'm doing instead of worrying about you."

She smiles against my shoulder. "Good," she breathes as she pulls away and cups my face in her hands. "I can't stand the thought of losing you, Logan Knight. Even though you've decided we can't be together, I still need to know you're on this earth. Even if it's not with me."

My heart cracks as her words hit me with full force. Lying here in this bed, knowing she's been by my side since I got here, I completely forgot about the morning before... about coming home and breaking her heart after her brother asked me to stay away from her.

I can't go against what he wants, but I can't let her go.

Not after all of this.

A soft knock sounds on the door and it slowly opens as August walks in. I forgot to tell my mom, but I guess she took it upon herself to tell him he could come in. Either that or he heard I was awake and wasn't able to wait any longer.

His eyes scan the two of us in bed, embracing one another, and I see his Adam's apple bob as he swallows hard. A wave of relief passes over his face and he smiles at me as he walks farther into the room. His hands are tucked in his front pockets and he shifts his weight nervously as his eyes meet mine.

"Welcome back." He smiles at me, nodding. "You gave us quite the scare, dude. I'm so fucking happy to see you awake."

I smile back at him, chuckling as Isla attempts to

move away from me, but I hold her closer. "I'm glad to be awake. I wasn't anticipating that shit and honestly, still can't believe it happened. But I'm here and on the mend."

"How long until you're back on the ice?" August questions me, curiosity and concern mixing in his irises as he sits down on the seat my mother was in before she left. "Actually, forget I asked that. None of that matters, as long as you're going to be okay and recover from this shit."

"No, you're right," I agree with him. "But I do wanna get back on the ice. The doctor said two to four weeks, just depends on when the neurologist clears me."

August nods, smiling at me as he chews on the inside of his cheek. He falls silent for a moment before directing his gaze to Isla. "Hey, sis, do you think you could give us a few minutes alone?"

My eyebrows draw together and she slowly sits up, my arms abruptly falling away from her. The tension rolls off her body and I can tell she's uncomfortable in this moment. "Sure," she offers quietly as she climbs off the bed. Ignoring her brother, she leans over, pressing her lips to the side of my head. "I'll be right out in the hall if you need me."

Her words warm my heart, like she thinks she

can protect me from him or something. I grab her hand and squeeze her warm palm before releasing her. Her smile is bright, her eyes soft as she looks at me once more before disappearing from the room, leaving August and I alone.

The silence is heavy and an awkwardness hangs in the air before he speaks. "I was wrong."

Squinting my eyes, I meet his regretful gaze. "About what?"

"You and Isla," he says quietly, his eyes dropping down to his hands in his lap. "I was just so fucking mad and hurt by the whole situation that I wasn't thinking about it clearly. But after your accident, I don't know, it opened my eyes and I was able to see that I was wrong all along."

Adjusting myself in the bed, I sit up farther, my head pounding in protest against my movements, but I ignore the pain as I focus on August. He looks back up at me, a small frown on his face as his eyes desperately search mine.

"You're the one who makes her happy." His voice is soft and warm, the guilt hanging heavily in his admission. "I was wrong to say you would end up like your dad and that you would hurt her. I see it now, what I was trying to ignore all along. The two of you belong together and honestly, I can't think of someone more deserving of her."

"Are you sure you're not just saying that because I'm lying in a hospital bed right now?" I ask him, jokingly, as I smile at him.

August chuckles, rolling his eyes. "That might have something to do with it." He pauses, his face falling serious as he stares back at me. "I mean it, though, Logan. Please forgive me for being a fucking asshole and trying to come between the two of you. I honestly can't imagine her with anyone but you."

"You don't have to ask for my forgiveness." I'm nothing but honest with him right now and a little taken aback by his change of heart. "I promise you I won't hurt her. This isn't just a little fling. This is a forever kind of thing."

August smiles back at me. "I see that now. But what kind of brother would I be if I didn't threaten bodily harm on you for hurting her?"

We both break out into laughter as August rises to his feet, his hand clasping my shoulder. "Let me go get your girl. And I'll see you when you get out of this place."

I nod, smiling at my best friend as he turns away to go get Isla from the hallway. He disappears and Isla comes walking back through the door a few moments later. Her eyes are hesitant as they search mine with a wariness.

"Is everything okay?" she questions me, her voice quiet as she sits down on the edge of the bed.

I smile up at her. "Everything's perfect." With my hands, I motion for her to come back to me and she brings her legs onto the bed, scooting closer to me as she lies on her side beside me. She wraps her arm around my waist and I hold her close with my arm around her shoulders. "Can you do something for me, baby?"

"Anything," she whispers as she lifts her head and rolls onto her stomach slightly, sliding her hands against my chest before propping her chin on them.

"Be mine?"

Her brown eyes bounce back and forth, rapidly searching mine. "That's what you want?"

"More than anything in the world."

I watch as her face transforms, her lips curling upward into a grin, and her body slides against mine as she moves closer, her hands cupping the sides of my face. "I've always been yours, Logan Knight, ever since we were kids." She pauses, the pads of her thumbs slowly stroking my cheeks. "You've just been too stupid to realize it."

"I hope you know I'm never going to let you go now."

"Good." She brings her lips to mine, warm and soft brushing against mine. "Because I wouldn't let you, even if you tried."

EPILOGUE
ISLA

ONE YEAR LATER

Standing beside the frozen lake, I watch Logan as he effortlessly skates around. He makes it look as if it's so easy, like it's second nature to him. I learned how to ice skate when I was a kid; since I was always at the rink and with my dad being a retired NHL player, I didn't have much choice but to join in with them.

It's been years since I've actually skated now, though, and the ice that covers the frozen pond is nowhere near as smooth as the ice they have at the rink.

"What's wrong, baby?" Logan questions me as

he skates over and skids to a stop in front of me. "Don't tell me you forgot how to skate."

I narrow my eyes at him, standing on the gravel path beside the lake. "No... it's just been a while and I don't really want to fall."

Logan holds his hand out to me, a smile playing on his lips. "Let me help you. I promise to catch you if you fall," he adds with a wink.

I slide my hand into his and let him lead me onto the ice. Unlike him, I can't just run and skate without missing a beat. I look like a child, stepping onto it with unsteady feet and weak ankles. My grip tightens on Logan's as I attempt to glide across it, like him.

He doesn't let go of my hand, slowly skating beside me as I work my legs back and forth in an attempt to slide across the ice. It's almost like riding a bike and the motion comes back to me quickly, even though I'm still rusty. And, to be honest, I would rather pretend like I don't feel comfortable doing it by myself if it means he'll keep holding my hand.

After Logan's accident last year, we were finally able to make things official. We didn't have to hide behind closed doors and keep our relationship a secret. He made sure everyone knew I was his girl, even if he did get a little jealous and overprotective at times.

August adjusted better than I thought and instead of being weird toward us, he just liked to talk a lot of shit and crack jokes all the time, like we were his source of entertainment. We made sure to make it super uncomfortable for him when he was being a dick and didn't shy away from any PDA.

To be frank, Logan couldn't keep his hands off me and I loved every damn minute of it.

He's halfway into his senior year of college with me in my sophomore year now. Different scouts have already approached him, wanting to draft him onto their teams. He is set to fly out next week to go visit a few of their training camps, because he needed to make sure he was making the best decision before choosing a team to play for.

And it was helpful with Camilla being his agent. Even though she is his mom, she still treats him like she does all of her other clients and goes to bat for him like no one else. If there is anyone who is going to make sure he gets the best deal possible and is fully taken care of, it's her.

I'm happy for him because he's getting to live his dream. Since he was a little boy, he envisioned playing for the NHL and now it was finally coming true. Even though I'm worried for our future, there's no way I would be the one to stand between him and his dream. I will support him through everything, even if it means we have to spend some time apart.

Nothing will ever come between us again.

"Okay, I think I got this," I tell Logan, letting go of his hand as I begin to skate on my own. He skates backward with me, watching as my muscle memory kicks in and I begin to slide across the ice like I remember doing as a kid. Logan smiles at me, his grin infectious as he goes over and grabs two sticks and a puck.

He skates back over to me, handing me one as he drops the puck on the ice. "Like old times?" His bright blue eyes stare directly through mine.

I smile back, holding the stick in both hands. "Try and get it from me," I taunt him, taking the puck as I begin to skate. When we were kids, he, August, and Hayden used to force me to play with them because they needed a fourth player. I was never really any good, but now that I'm back at it, it's coming back to me like I remembered it.

Logan smirks, slowly skating toward me, the blade of his stick sliding across the ice. I move the puck away from him twice, before he eventually connects with it and slaps it away from me. I look up at him, narrowing my eyes, but the side of his lips curl up in a smirk and he drops his stick onto the ice.

I pause, slowly sliding to a stop as I raise an eyebrow at him. Logan pushes off on his skates, coming directly toward me with his arms outstretched. He collides into me, wrapping them around me as he laughs and I yelp. Except, he doesn't hold me up like he intends and knocks me onto the ice, falling down on top of me.

"What the hell, Logan!" I yell out at him, my voice drowned out by his laughter. His bright eyes shine down at me and he laughs like he thinks it's the funniest thing. It's infectious and I find myself laughing along with him as we lay on the cold ice together.

"Hey, I promised I would catch you if you fell." He smiles, his eyes burning holes through mine as he cups the side of my face with his gloved hand. "It just so happens that I fell with you... so fucking hard."

Logan rolls off me and climbs onto his skates before reaching down for me. He lifts me up with him, making sure I'm steady on my feet. He takes my hands in his as I tilt my head back to get lost in the oceanic depths of his eyes. "Come with me."

My eyebrows draw together as my heart pounds erratically in my chest. "Come with you where?"

"Wherever I go." His voice is soft, but his eyes are pleading. "I don't want to live life without you, Isla. I can't stand the thought of being away from you. I know it's a lot to ask, but I want you to come with me, to be by my side, wherever that may be."

My eyes widen as I watch him slowly lower himself in front of me, dropping to one knee on the ice. He releases one of my hands, reaching into the zipper pocket of his coat before he pulls out a black velvet box.

My heart crawls into my throat and tears prick the corners of my eyes as Logan lifts his gaze back to mine.

"Be my wife, baby girl," he murmurs, flipping the lid of the box open, revealing a white gold band with a single diamond on top. I don't bother fully looking at the ring, because I can't tear my eyes away from his. "You're the only teammate that matters to me—that I want to spend the rest of my life with. Will you marry me, Isla Whitley?"

Tears fill my eyes as I stare down at the love of my life kneeling before me. I've loved him for as long as I can remember, and now he's asking me to be his for the rest of our days.

"Yes," I breathe, a smile consuming my lips as he pulls the glove from my hand. He drops it down onto the ice beside him and pulls the ring from the velvet box before sliding it along my ring finger.

"You're it for me, baby," he smiles, rising to his feet as he wraps his hands around my waist. I link my arms around the back of his neck. "When I envision my future, you're all I see. You're all I want."

"I've always been yours, Logan." I get lost in the waves that crash in his ocean eyes, tears of happiness streaming down the sides of my face. "And I want nothing more than to spend the rest of my days with you, by your side, with your last name."

He brings his face down to mine, his lips brushing against mine. "'Til death do us part, baby girl."

I'm completely consumed by him as he claims my mouth with his, breathing me in as he drains my lungs of oxygen. My brain swims and I'm so lost in him. In my fiancé.

The one I've loved since we were kids.

The one who I will happily spend the rest of my life with as his wife.

Logan fucking Knight.

LOGAN AND ISLA BONUS SCENE

The water ripples along the shore as we walk hand in hand through the sand. The weather in Jamaica is a complete contrast from Vermont. Isla seems to enjoy it and I just enjoy her, so it's a win-win. I would be lying if I said I didn't miss the colder temperatures I'm used to. And the feeling of the ice beneath my feet.

Isla stops, a sigh slipping from her lips as I release her hand and wrap my arm around her shoulder. We walked out onto the beach after we finished our dinner to watch the sunset. The night has grown darker now as the moon has risen and replaced the sunlight from above.

Tilting my head, I look down at her and a smile touches my lips. I love this girl so much it fucking hurts. Her wavy hair is tousled and tangled from the Caribbean breeze. She turns to look up at me, her face sun-kissed and tanner than I've ever seen on her before.

My arm falls away from her shoulders and I take her hands in mine, running my thumb over the two rings on her finger. I'll never forget the day she officially became my wife. The way her white dress hugged every curve, flowing out around her feet as she walked down the aisle to me.

We got married on a fall day at the lake where I proposed, surrounded by all of our friends and family. Isla is beautiful, but that day, she literally stole the air from my lungs. If I could live that day over again, I would, but I love this future we're building together. And I can't wait to start a family with my beautiful wife.

A mischievous grin tugs at the corners of my lips as I look past Isla and glance around the beach. There's not a single person in sight. The resort was having some kind of party tonight, so I imagine that most of the guests are there. Which leaves Isla and I alone on the white sandy beach.

"What are you up to?"

I glance down at my wife. "Nothing, baby." I

smirk, releasing her hands as I take a step away from her.

"I know that smile, Logan," she says, her voice playful as she narrows her eyes. "And I don't like it."

With my back to the water, I slowly start to walk backward into it. It's warm as the small ripples move around my ankles. "I don't know what you're talking about," I tell her, a chuckle vibrating in my chest.

Isla watches me from where she's standing on the beach. As I stop in the water, I grab the bottom hem of my shirt and peel it off, tossing it to her. Her eyes widen as I slide my hands under the waistband of my pants and begin to push them down.

"Logan Knight," she scolds me, her voice hushed. "Don't you do it."

I can't fight the grin as I watch her face shift between anger and amusement. Stripping myself of my clothes, I toss my shorts and boxer briefs to her as I stand naked in the water. Isla drops my clothes onto the sand and her footsteps are quick as she comes up to attempt to cover me up.

"There's no one here but us," I tell her, grabbing her hips as I spin her around. Dipping my head down to her neck, I press my lips against her skin as I begin to push down the straps of her dress. "No one can see us right now, Isla. Come skinny-dipping with me."

Isla turns around to face me, her eyes searching mine. The moonlight casts itself across her face, revealing her pink cheeks. She looks fucking delectable with her hair a mess and the straps of her dress halfway down her arms.

"What if someone sees us?" she half whispers, the innocence evident in her gaze. My heart swells, knowing that this is just another first for her and she's doing it with me.

"Fuck them," I answer her, hooking my fingers under the neckline of her dress as I begin to push it down. Her chest rises and falls with every shallow breath as she lets me strip her of her clothing. It isn't long before we're standing naked together, ankle deep in the warm Caribbean water.

Isla takes a step toward me, wrapping her arms around the back of my neck. A smirk tugs on the corners of her lips and she matches my energy, not giving a fuck about anyone other than the two of us in this moment. Grabbing her waist, I pull her to me as my face dips down to hers.

Our mouths collide and her lips instantly part, granting me access inside. My tongue slides across hers, tangling together as we deepen the kiss.

There's a shift, the tension heavy between us. There's nothing sweet about the way our mouths melt together. Instead, it's fueled purely by need and desire. It's borderline feral as she slides her hands up the back of my head, gripping my locks of hair.

Releasing her waist, I slide my hands along her torso, only stopping as I reach where her buttocks meet her thighs. Cupping her ass, I grip her flesh as I hoist her up into my arms. She lets out a yelp, but I swallow the sound as I keep my lips glued to hers. My cock is as hard as a rock and it throbs against her, feeling her wet pussy pressed to my stomach as she wraps her legs around my waist.

Turning around, I hold her in my arms, our tongues still dancing together as I walk us deeper into the water. It's warm against my skin and the waves are gentle as they lap against our bodies. I continue walking until the water is just above my waist. Still holding her up, I slide my hands to her hips as I break away.

Isla is breathless, her eyes burning through mine. "Why'd you stop?"

"Lay back for me, baby," I murmur, pulling her away slightly as I shift her lower, my cock pressing against her pussy. "I wanna fuck you under the moonlight."

"In the ocean?" she breathes, wiggling her hips as the tip of my cock breaches her center. She's wet and slick, tighter than ever as I slowly ease inside her.

"In the ocean," I groan, lifting her up and down as I stroke my length with her pussy. "Lay back, baby. I won't let you go."

Isla slowly releases her hands from my hair, sliding them down my arms as she lowers herself into the water. Her hair fans out in the ocean, like a halo around her head as she lays flat on her back. She floats on top of the water, her legs wrapped around my waist as I hold her by the hips. The water ripples across her breasts and I'm mesmerized by the sight of her like this.

Holding on to her, I shift my hips, thrusting my cock in and out of her. Slow and sweet is my method of torture. Isla pushes her arms through the water, letting them float beside her as I begin to fuck her harder. This is an image I will gladly burn into my memory. One that I will hold on to until the day I leave this earth.

Keeping one hand on her hip, I slide the other to her center, pressing my fingers between our bodies as we continue to meet in the middle. My thumb brushes against her clit and her hips buck slightly. I work my finger around the small bundle of nerves, applying pressure as I move it in a circular motion.

Isla's legs tighten around my waist as I piston my hips, fucking her harder with every thrust. She's breathless, moans slipping from her lips as I pound into her. Her pussy begins to tighten around my cock as I continue to play with her clit, and I know that she's getting close. That alone has me on the brink of coming.

A warmth spreads through my stomach before consuming my entire body as my balls constrict, drawing closer with my release. Isla cries out as she comes undone, shattering into a million pieces around my cock. That's all it takes to have me falling into the abyss with her. Thrusting harder into her, I lose myself deep in her pussy, filling her to the brim.

We ride out our high, both of us completely breathless as Isla continues to float on her back in the water. I slowly pull out of her and she releases her legs from my waist as I turn her body in the water. Bending my knees, I dip down under the water, sliding my hands behind the backs of her knees and her shoulders.

Isla wraps her arms around my neck as I lift her into the air, both of our bodies wet and salty. She turns her head to look at me, her eyes meeting mine under the moonlight. "You never cease to surprise me, Logan. I love you."

A smile tugs on the corners of my lips as I stare back at my beautiful wife. "I love you."

Leaving the water, I carry Isla back to the beach to retrieve our clothes. We're both drenched from our dip in the ocean, but neither of us care as we walk back to the main part of the resort. We walk together, hand in hand.

In this moment and every one to come.

Isla Knight will always be my entire fucking world.

NEXT IN THE SERIES

Deflected Hearts is the second book from the Wyncote Wolves, featuring August and Poppy. Continue reading on the next page for a look inside Deflected Hearts.

PROLOGUE
POPPY

Life has always been a series of ups and downs for me. I came from a broken home, having to divide holidays between two households after my parents divorced when I was ten years old. It was a weird adjustment at the time, especially when I was just entering my teenage years. There are so many things that you're experiencing mentally and physically, and then throw in a divorce and it's a perfect triangle of self-despair.

After what I had experienced with my parents, I made a promise to myself that I would never do the same to my children as they did to my sister, Evie, and I. I wouldn't have a child, only to have our family and lives fall to shambles.

Evie struggled with it the worst. We were

sixteen months apart, so we were close, but we were polar opposites. I was the quiet one, where she was the one who was the life of the party. She began to act out as we entered high school and wound up in trouble more times than I could count. She blamed my parents for separating and remarrying, instead of trying to work things out and have our family be together.

It was the summer before my senior year of high school when we lost her. Evie was set to leave for college at the end of the summer and there was an annual party thrown at one of the lakes in town. She had just gotten into a fight with our stepmother and father that night and drank more than she should.

It was late at night and Evie had the great idea for everyone to go swimming. A few of the other kids agreed with her, but I begged her not to do it. To just let me take her home, where she was safe, but she refused. We were staying at our dad's house that weekend and she told me she never wanted to go back there again.

That night, she got her wish.

Evie dove into the lake, not realizing that the area was shallow and there were jagged rocks just beneath the surface. Her head collided with one, effectively snapping her neck from the force. I watched her do it and then float to the surface, face-down. Everyone else was too drunk to realize what was going on as I dragged her onto the shore, screaming for help.

Losing her completely turned my world upside down. There were so many what-ifs that hung heavily in the air. My father never quite got over it, especially after the fight they had that night before she passed. He partially blamed me for not preventing it from happening, even though I had tried.

It rocked everyone's lives and to be honest, I'm not quite sure that any of us truly got over her death. I know that I didn't and the guilt still consumed me from time to time. Maybe my father was right. If I would have tried harder, I could have stopped her from diving in. I live with that every day of my life, because not only did I lose my sister, but I lost my best friend too.

My footsteps are light and dread rolls in the pit of my stomach as I pace up and down the short hallway in my apartment. I glance at my phone, looking at the timer as it begins to count down from ten seconds. The anxiety runs through my system and there's nothing I can do to control it in this moment.

PROLOGUE

The alarm begins to sound and a ragged breath leaves my lips as I silence it and slide it into the front pocket of my hoodie. I can't believe this is happening right now—that I've gotten myself into a situation like this one, of all things.

My hand finds the doorknob and I slowly turn it as I walk back into the bathroom. I had it closed, as if that would really make a difference. Inhaling deeply, my footsteps are slow as I walk over to the counter. I close my eyes for a moment, wishing for it not to be what I think it's going to be. As I open them, I finally look down at the plastic stick sitting by the sink.

My stomach sinks as my heart crawls into my throat. Two little blue lines stare back at me and it feels as if the rug is being ripped from beneath my feet.

I'm pregnant.

And alone.

The one thing that I never wanted to happen is happening. It would be different if things would have worked out between him and I, but they didn't. He didn't form attachments, and now I'm carrying his baby inside me. A baby that is going to be raised in a broken home, just like I promised myself I would never do.

PROLOGUE

A sob tears through me, the tears instantly springing from my eyes as I sink onto the bathroom floor. It's been four years since Evie's death and right now, I need her more than anything. She would know exactly what to say or what to do.

I miss my sister… my best friend.

But the only person I have right now is myself.

And August Whitley's baby.

ACKNOWLEDGMENTS

My husband was a HUGE inspiration behind even beginning this series. When we first met, he played hockey (and played since he was a kid). Thank you for answering my never-ending questions and helping me to construct some of the scenes. And for being more inspiration than just the hockey parts ;)

Thank you to Christina who practically runs my life and is always there to listen to me freak out and talk me off the ledge. I love youuuuu.

Thank you to my beta readers: Bre, Megan & Rita. The three of you read this when it was trash and helped me sift through it all.

Thank you to Rumi for helping make this shine. And for loving Logan and Isla along the way. AND for being by my side since day one.

Thank you to my proof babes: Jamie & Brenda. You two have the ability to pick out things that I miss and I appreciate it so much!

Thank you to my Ramziti. You pushed me to do this when I was filled with so much doubt. You're always by my side and cheering for me. I love you long time.

Thank you to my twin bitch, Cass. You always slay the covers and I can't put our friendship into words. I'm gonna say it and you better not hate me for it... HUGS.

Thank you to my Cat. You're so magical with your ability and this alternate cover is to die for. I love your face.

And thank you to all of my author friends who are my forever sprinting buddies. I wouldn't have been able to write all of these words without your support and constant pushing. (You all know who you are and my brain sucks and I don't want to forget anyone if I try to list you all out.)

ALSO BY CALI MELLE

WYNCOTE WOLVES SERIES

Cross Checked Hearts

Deflected Hearts

Playing Offsides

The Faceoff

The Goalie Who Stole Christmas

Splintered Ice

Coast to Coast

Off-Ice Collision

ABOUT THE AUTHOR

Cali Melle is a contemporary romance author who loves writing stories that will pull at your heartstrings. You can always expect her stories to come fully equipped with heartthrobs and a happy ending, along with some steamy scenes and some sports action. In her free time, Cali can usually be found spending time with her family or with her nose in a book. As a hockey and figure skating mom, you can probably find her freezing at an ice rink watching her kids.

Printed in Great Britain
by Amazon

24462191R10189